snowdrops & winterberry

OTHER BOOKS AND AUDIOBOOKS BY SARAH M. EDEN

The Lancaster Family

Seeking Persephone
Courting Miss Lancaster
Romancing Daphne
Loving Lieutenant Lancaster
*Christmas at Falstone Castle**
also in *All Hearts Come Home for Christmas* anthology
Charming Artemis

The Gents

Forget Me Not
Snowdrops and Winterberry
(previously titled *The Holly and the Ivy* in *The Holly and the Ivy* anthology)*
Lily of the Valley
Fleur-de-Lis

The Huntresses

*The Best-Laid Plans**
The Best Intentions
The Best of Friends

The Jonquil Brothers

The Kiss of a Stranger
Friends and Foes
Drops of Gold
As You Are
A Fine Gentleman
For Love or Honor
The Heart of a Vicar
Charming Artemis

Stand-Alones

Glimmer of Hope
An Unlikely Match
For Elise
The Fiction Kitchen Trio Cookbook

*Novella

CHRONOLOGICAL ORDER OF ALL RELATED SARAH M. EDEN GEORGIAN- & REGENCY-ERA BOOKS

Forget Me Not
*Snowdrops and Winterberry (The Holly and the Ivy)**
Lily of the Valley
Fleur-de-Lis
Seeking Persephone
Courting Miss Lancaster
Glimmer of Hope
Romancing Daphne
The Kiss of a Stranger
Friends and Foes
Drops of Gold
For Elise
As You Are
A Fine Gentleman
For Love or Honor
Loving Lieutenant Lancaster
*Christmas at Falstone Castle**
The Heart of a Vicar
The Best-Laid Plans
Charming Artemis
The Best Intentions
The Best of Friends

A Gents Christmas Novella with a Bonus Epilogue

SARAH M. EDEN

Covenant Communications, Inc.

Cover image credit: Adobe Stock

Published by Covenant Communications, Inc.
American Fork, Utah

This is a work of fiction. The characters, names, incidents, places, and dialogue are either products of the author's imagination, and are not to be construed as real, or are used fictitiously.

Library of Congress Cataloging-in-Publication Data

Name: Sarah M. Eden
Title: The Holly and the Ivy / Sarah M. Eden
Description: American Fork, UT : Covenant Communications, Inc. [2024]
Identifiers: Library of Congress Control Number 2024934781 | ISBN: 978-1-52442-716-0
LC record available at https://lccn.loc.gov/2024934781

Printed in the United States of America
First Printing: October 2024

30 29 28 27 26 25 24 10 9 8 7 6 5 4 3 2 1

Chapter One

March 1786

FALSTONE CASTLE HAD BEEN EXTREMELY quiet for the past few months. The late Duke of Kielder had died four months earlier. His son, Adam, a mere seven years old at the time, had been sent to live near Harrow School. The widowed duchess, as always, was away, traveling and spending time elsewhere. Robbie MacGregor had found the silence intolerable. She was not one who preferred chaos and noise, but the quiet was disconcerting because it served as a reminder that her time as nursemaid to the young duke was coming to a close.

Adam, now only just turned eight, was too young to be at Harrow and was living in a nearby boardinghouse specifically for wee boys whose families had sent them away before their schooltime was meant to begin. They lived there on the same schedule as the older boys who were attending Harrow, and their days were filled with lessons and schooling, like those of their older counterparts. It was both a school and a substitute home for boys who were far too young for either one. Adam would not be at Falstone Castle often anymore. And when he was, he was at the age when a governess was a far more fitting choice than a nursemaid.

Robbie was accustomed to the need to find new employment when the wee bairns she looked after outgrew their need for her. Indeed, before his passing, the late duke had indicated she ought to begin that search again. He and his wife had been estranged nearly all of Adam's life, and it had been unlikely that there'd be more children in the castle to look after. Now that Adam was fatherless, it was a guarantee.

She cared about all the little ones she'd looked after over the years, but Adam held a special place in her heart. His life had been difficult, torn between two parents who were forever at odds with each other, desperate to please them both but not having the first idea how. He was quiet and shy but also deeply curious and had a heart that, while guarded, was tender and compassionate. She'd been concerned about him before his father's passing; she was full worried for him now.

But a ray of hope had arrived a week before Adam's return from his first school term break: a letter from Brier Hill, a small estate about a day's drive from Falstone Castle. Lord and Lady Jonquil were inviting Adam to spend his school holiday with them. The young couple had met him during the last ball held at Falstone Castle before the old duke's passing. They were kind and had taken a particular interest in him. They'd sent him letters, asking how he was, expressing their sorrow at his grief. Adam was wary of strangers, but Robbie suspected this visit would do him a heap of good.

She stepped inside the master's bedchamber. The duchess had insisted Adam take up residence there after his father's death, pulling him from the nursery that had once been his domain. Robbie'd been in no position to deny the order, but how she wished Adam's mother could see how unhappy he was in this space. It, no doubt, reminded him painfully of his father. And the room was far too large for an eight-year-old boy. The servants had had to find a box for him to stand on simply to get into the bed. The dressing table, the washbasin, even the windows, were set too high for him. The room stood as a stark reminder of what Adam had lost and the burden his tiny shoulders now carried.

He sat in an armchair near the fireplace, dressed in the black of mourning, bent over a book. She wished it were a lighthearted book, the sort most wee'uns read at his age. He'd taken far too much to heart his role as the Duke of Kielder and the master of this castle. He'd become ever more quiet and withdrawn, and he never seemed happy. That change, in particular, fair broke her heart.

She had, under strict orders from the duchess, sent a scared, innocent little boy off to a cold and uncaring boardinghouse to undertake schooling instead of remaining at the castle, surrounded by people who cared about him. He had returned harder and more unhappy and, in many ways, unreachable.

"Well then, my wee Adam, it's time we were off."

He closed his book on his lap. His posture remained quite rigid, quite formal. That had become his way while he was gone. He'd never been the easy, relaxed child others were, but this degree of feigned maturity was new for him.

"I'm not certain I want to go." His imperious tone would likely fool many people into thinking he was stubborn and autocratic. Robbie knew him too well to believe such a thing. Her wee Adam was scared.

"Lady Jonquil said in her invitation that she very much wishes to see you. Disappointing a lady is nae a gentlemanly thing to do." Robbie had discovered in the single day Adam had been home that he responded more to appeals to his ideas about the correct way for a duke to act than he did to anything else.

His little mouth twisted, pulling at the spiderweb of scars that marred the right side of his face. The sweet boy had been born with a stump of an ear and had endured far too many procedures undertaken by different surgeons. That they had butchered him would be obvious for the rest of his life.

"Would my father have gone to Brier Hill if Lord and Lady Jonquil had invited him?" Adam asked.

Robbie nodded. "He would have, aye, especially if they'd written to him as often as Lord and Lady Jonquil have written to you."

"But what if they don't really want me to visit? What if they are only asking because they think they're supposed to?" There was a wee inkling of the uncertain and tenderhearted little Adam she had loved so much these past eight years.

"I do nae think they'd have invited you if they weren't anxious to see you."

"But that would be ridiculous."

Robbie had to bite back a smile at the all-too-familiar word. Adam had adopted "*ridiculous*" as his favorite descriptor several months earlier. "Why, wee boy, would that be ridiculous?"

"I only met them once. I'm not their friend. I'm not their son. Mothers and fathers want their children to visit at term break." His countenance fell a little. "Most do, leastwise."

The poor bairn. He was well aware his mother hadn't sent for him to spend his term break with her.

Robbie sat on the ottoman placed in front of the chair that engulfed this tiny boy and his enormous burdens. "I think they should very much like to have you visit. They would not have written to you if they did not like you and want to have you come to Brier Hill."

He sat for a moment, thinking. "People do like to have dukes visit."

"Dukes are sought-after guests, aye." Oh, how she wished he understood he was more than a duke. But if leaning on that meant he would undertake this visit, she was willing to go along. He needed to be away from this castle, away from the reminder of his father's death and his mother's defection. He needed a term break filled with something happy and uplifting before returning to the boardinghouse, where she suspected he'd been terribly unhappy.

Adam gave a firm, regal nod of his head. He slid off the chair. How tiny he looked in this enormous room.

"We had best go," he said, his little eight-year-old voice sounding far too old.

Robbie held out her hand to him. He didn't take it but walked with a ramrod posture from the room. He had once clung to her hand like any little one would. That too had changed while he was away.

She ought to be encouraging the separation, knowing it was only a matter of time before the duchess chose to let Robbie go and hire a governess. But this wee lad, with his high rank and his low spirits, needed her. He was hurting and alone. If she were gone, he would slip further and further away.

Dukes weren't supposed to be scared. Adam knew a great deal about what dukes were and weren't supposed to be, what they were and weren't supposed to do. His father had taught him. And Adam was a good learner.

But as the traveling carriage approached Brier Hill, he *was* scared. He'd never visited anyone before. He had experience welcoming people to Falstone Castle. Father used to hold balls there so Mother would come home. Adam would stand with them as they greeted their guests. He knew how to do that.

But this was the first time he had been a guest somewhere else. Before this, the only time he had ever left home was when he was sent to the boardinghouse next to Harrow. And that had been a miserable thing. Would this be as well? Adam was so tired of being miserable.

Were dukes supposed to be miserable? Father had never told him that, but Father hadn't always been happy. Maybe that was one of the rules: a duke worked hard, looked after people, was very responsible, and didn't get to be happy.

There were so many reasons Adam didn't want to be a duke. The biggest one, of course, was that he wouldn't be one if his father were still alive. He missed his father. He refused to miss his mother.

The coachman opened the door of the carriage, and Adam held his breath.

"We'd best step down, wee Adam." Nurse Robbie had made the journey with him. Dukes probably weren't supposed to need nursemaids, but having her with him helped him be brave. And dukes *were* meant to be brave.

He accepted the coachman's hand as he climbed onto the step, but only because he was too short to do it on his own. Someday he'd be bigger.

Nurse Robbie followed close behind as he walked toward the front door of Brier Hill. He wished she could walk beside him, hold his hand like she used to. But he needed to act like a duke and not like a baby.

He'd not quite reached the front door when a tall gentleman with wavy golden hair bounded from the house. Though Adam had met him only once, he recognized Lord Jonquil. He'd bounced about the entryway of Falstone Castle all those months ago, looking like someone who wanted very much to run down a corridor but had been told that corridors were not the place for playing. Adam didn't know any grown people quite like him.

Adam set one arm at his stomach and pointed his foot out, but he couldn't remember where his other arm was meant to go when he bowed. At his side? Behind his back? He was making a poor showing for himself. He guessed at the position of his arm and hoped he was at least close to correct. "Lord Jonquil, thank you for your invitation." He had heard some of his father's exalted guests say that when they'd arrived at the castle. It seemed the right thing to say now.

Lord Jonquil returned the bow with a perfectly executed one. Adam studied it, wanting to know how to do better. The arm he'd not known what to do with was supposed to stick out at the side. He told himself to remember that. He also watched how low Lord Jonquil bowed since that was supposed to be important. Dukes didn't bow as low to other people as those people bowed to dukes.

"We are very pleased you chose to accept," Lord Jonquil said. "But I feel I must issue a warning."

Worry immediately seized Adam's heart. Was he going to be sent away? Were there other guests here? Was he not actually wanted?

In a voice that sounded like he had a great secret to share, Lord Jonquil said, "My wife is giddy at the idea of having you here. She will be here to greet you any moment and may not be able to prevent herself from squealing with delight, perhaps even hugging you."

Adam swallowed against the lump of uncertainty forming in his throat. "She will hug me?"

Lord Jonquil shrugged and grinned. "She might. Your visit is all she has talked about for weeks."

Adam could feel his face scrunch between his eyes. Why would she be so happy to have him visit? Adam's father had liked to spend time with him, but his mother certainly didn't. Nurse Robbie never forgot about him, which meant she probably liked being with him. Jeb, who worked in the stables at Falstone Castle, never seemed grumpy because Adam was there. But only those three people. Lady Jonquil was probably happy about having a duke at her house. Mother often talked about the important people she spent time with. Being a duke made a person important.

He straightened his posture and made his face as fierce as his father's was when greeting people at the castle. Dukes were not meant to be frivolous, Father had often told him. Being serious was necessary.

"Lord Jonquil," Adam said, motioning to Nurse Robbie, "this is Nurse Robbie. She came here with me."

Lord Jonquil offered her a bow as well. Adam wasn't certain servants were usually bowed to. There was so much he didn't understand. With Father gone and Mother always away, there was no one to explain any of it to him.

A moment later, a lady stepped out the door. He knew her. He had never before met someone with hair the color of hers. It was brown and red at the same time. He found it very fascinating. He'd asked Lady Jonquil about it when he'd met her at Falstone Castle. She hadn't laughed at him for not knowing about red hair. And she didn't put the white powder in her hair like many ladies did. He didn't know why.

The very first letter he'd received after Father died had come from her. And she had written to him many times since. He was glad Lady Jonquil was happy to have him visit, even if it was just because he was a duke. He knew she would be kind to him; not many people were anymore.

"Oh! You've arrived at last!"

He watched her, uncertain. "Are you going to hug me?"

She smiled. "Not if you would rather I didn't."

He shook his head. Nurse Robbie sometimes hugged him. His father had now and then. He wasn't certain he wanted anyone else to.

Lady Jonquil didn't look angry. "And what would you like us to call you while you're here?"

"At school, they call me Your Grace or the duke."

She bent so they were looking right at each other instead of her looking down at him. "But is that what you want *us* to call you?"

He was confused. "I can choose?"

She nodded. "While you are here, we will do everything we can to make this a happy place for you. If that means not hugging you, we won't. If that means calling you Your Grace or Adam or whatever you wish, we will do so."

Dukes were supposed to be called Your Grace. That was one of the rules. And yet the idea of choosing something else caused a little bubble of something to push on his heart. Adam looked down at his feet for just a moment. "My father used to call me Adam."

Lord Jonquil said, "My father calls me Lucas, even though I have a title. Sometimes it's nice to have someone remember *who* you are and not merely *what* you are."

Adam looked up and directly into the eyes of Lady Jonquil. He didn't know why, but something about the way she looked at him made him want to cry. But dukes didn't cry.

"You can call me Adam," he said but made sure to sound very duke-like when he said it.

Lady Jonquil smiled, and it made his heart bounce around. "Welcome to Brier Hill, Adam."

Chapter Two

Howard Simpkin came from a family of builders. For generations, the Simpkins had lent their skills to building homes and shops and even the restoration of the grand Beverley Minster. Howard had taken a different road. He was still a builder, but a builder of gardens.

His father had called him every sort of fool when he had first set out on this venture. But Howard had managed to make something of a name for himself in the north of England. He had designed greens in York, garden plots at vicarages. He had built gardening sheds and herb houses. He felt certain that if he could only catch the attention of someone with influence and importance, he could make a roaring success of this occupation he had invented.

Just such an opportunity had at last presented itself. A request had come from Lord Jonquil, the heir of the Earl of Lampton, to design and build a walled garden on his estate in Northumberland. Howard didn't know very much about Brier Hill, where Lord Jonquil lived, but he knew the area had fertile soil and could grow a lovely garden. He also knew Brier Hill was not a large estate, leastwise when compared with the fine and grand principle estates of the aristocracy. But the size of the job was not nearly as important as how well Howard did his work. If Lord Jonquil was pleased with the results, he would be more likely to recommend Howard to his friends, his fellow gentlemen, perhaps even his parents.

Howard arrived at Brier Hill on the appointed day. He presented himself at the servants' entrance, as that was what most fine households preferred, and was instructed by the housekeeper to wait beneath a specific tree for His Lordship.

He took the opportunity to survey the area. He was at the side of the house, which offered a lovely view of the nearby hills and mountains. The grass beneath his feet was thick and abundant, a good indication of quality soil. The back lawn was enclosed by a stone fence, which, while not unheard of, was unusual. It was entirely possible Lord Jonquil would wish his garden walls to also be built of stone. Howard would have to inquire as to the availability.

A man approached, a gentleman by his appearance, and one well-to-do. This, no doubt, was Lord Jonquil himself. Howard doffed his hat and dipped his head.

Lord Jonquil's smile was welcoming and friendly. "Simpkin?"

"Yes, m'lord."

Lord Jonquil extended his hand and shook Howard's firmly. "I have kept you waiting, I'm afraid. We have newly arrived guests, and I was assisting my wife in welcoming them."

Being kept waiting by a patron was not an unusual thing. Having a patron express regret at the inconvenience most certainly was.

"I'll show you the place where I've envisioned the garden"—Lord Jonquil motioned him toward the gate in the stone wall—"and you can tell me if I'm an utter hulver-head."

Howard blinked a few times.

Lord Jonquil laughed. "I should likely try to at least sound proper, instead of tossing out cant and ridiculousness. You'll discover Lady Jonquil is far better behaved than I."

Howard hadn't the first idea what to make of this aristocrat, with his easy grin and casual saunter.

They passed through the gate and into an expansive, neatly maintained lawn. A few trees created clumps of shade and beauty. Howard followed his potential patron to the back corner.

"Here," Lord Jonquil said. "This corner is not used for anything, and it has a nice view. I would like the garden to be walled for privacy, but I don't want to block out so much sunlight that the flowers won't grow."

Not all the people Howard worked for recognized the necessity of considering such things. "I don't think you'll struggle overly much with that. I can build the new walls a touch lower than the existing ones. That'll allow a bit of extra light. The flowers and plants what're needing more sun can be planted away from the walls so they'll not be in too much shadow."

Lord Jonquil nodded his approval. "I'd like it to be large enough for a walking path, a couple of benches for sitting, a few trees and shrubs, as well as a good many flowers."

"Your wife likes flowers, does she?"

"She does." He spoke the two words a little hesitantly. "But this garden is a wish of mine. I know it is an unusual interest for a man, but I've always liked nature: plants and flowers and the rich smell of earth. We have extensive gardens at Lampton Park, and I've missed them."

Howard had not met many men who shared his enjoyment of gardens. Most were somewhat indifferent or preferred gardens that were useful. To have found in his first patron of influence a gentleman who cared personally about the results was a stroke of luck. If the man was pleased, he was likely to talk about it, brag about it, invite others to come see a garden that mattered to him.

They walked around the area where Lord Jonquil wished for his garden to be. Howard asked every question he could think of. His patron asked many as well. This garden was meant to be a mixture of formal and inviting. It was meant to be walled while still needing sunlight. Lord Jonquil was not certain stone could be obtained that matched the existing stone of the wall. All those things would complicate the job.

"If you give me today," Howard said, "I'll take measurements and sketch up an idea for you."

Lord Jonquil nodded. "I look forward to seeing it. Do you need anything to accomplish that?"

"I travel with all I need. I've a coach I remade myself. Outwardly, it simply looks like a worn old traveling coach, but the inside is something of a home. I've equipment, paper, and pencil lead. I can have something ready for you in a few hours. Of course, that's assuming you don't mind having my coach on your property. It isn't an eyesore, I swear to you."

"I don't mind. And your horses can be stabled here."

Howard was fortunate to have found a potential patron who was not merely enthusiastic but also generous.

Out of the corner of his eye he caught sight of a young boy walking beside a woman dressed in the plain clothes of a servant but holding herself with more confidence than a mere chambermaid.

Lord Jonquil must've noticed where his gaze had shifted, because he explained, "Our guest, the young Duke of Kielder, and Miss MacGregor."

Weren't that a strange thing? The boy couldn't have been more than seven or eight years old and already a duke. Duke or not, young boys were rambunctious and often caused trouble. Heaven help Howard, having a little one about might very well set him behind schedule or wreak havoc on his work.

He couldn't afford for his work not to be his very best this time. His entire future depended on it.

He would keep an eye on this tiny duke. If there were so much as a spot of trouble, he'd have a talk with the woman looking after the boy.

Chapter Three

"But I don't understand the purpose." Adam had made that objection several times.

Lord and Lady Jonquil had suggested a number of games that any child would enjoy. Adam, as Robbie knew well, was not "any child." They were being very patient with him, but they were clearly baffled.

"The purpose of a bilboquet is . . . entertainment," Lord Jonquil said. "It's a challenge to try to catch the ball on the stick. The attempts often go hilariously wrong, making it humorous to try and also to watch."

"The purpose is to laugh at people?" Adam's dark brows pulled inward, and his wee mouth tensed into a tiny twist of lips.

"Not *at* people," Lord Jonquil was quick to say. "*With* people, certainly."

Robbie sat a bit apart from the couple and her little charge. Nursemaids weren't meant to participate in these things, but the situation was an unusual one. Adam was visiting without a parent, and he hadn't a governess—yet. He was left to navigate this uncharted territory without the usual support. Ought she to intervene? To explain a bit more about Adam?

His expression remained hard. "Sometimes people are laughing *at* someone even though they say they aren't."

"That won't happen here," Lady Jonquil said. "We would never permit it."

Wariness remained on that little face. Robbie's heart broke to see it. He'd always been a cautious boy, but the past months had turned his vigilance to fear. Too many people had disappointed and abandoned him. He expected it now.

"Do show him how to use the bilboquet, Lucas," Lady Jonquil said to her husband.

While Lord Jonquil demonstrated, his wife rose from her chair and crossed to sit beside Robbie. "Has he truly never played with a bilboquet? I thought most children had."

"I'll not speak ill of the late duke," Robbie said, "but I will tell you that Falstone Castle was a solemn place while this duke was a wee thing. He had a few toys, but not many. And his departed father was nae one for games and such, so our wee duke didn't learn to enjoy them."

"Ah." Lady Jonquil nodded. "Hence, the reason he couldn't fathom the purpose of the toy. He did not grow up realizing that toys don't need a 'purpose' other than enjoyment."

"I did try to teach him," Robbie said.

Lady Jonquil gave her a reassuring smile. "I am absolutely certain you did."

They were a generous-hearted couple. Robbie had realized that straight off.

"Do you suppose Adam would be more inclined to play if he thought the toy he was playing with had some educational value or strategy to its use?"

"Aye. 'Tis how I convinced him to learn chess and draughts. The strategy of them are good for the mind, he decided." A hint of sadness touched her as she thought back on those discussions. How she wished he could have been a lighthearted little boy. The weight of a title and responsibilities had landed on him far too soon, and he'd lost his chance at being a child.

During this conversation, Adam had been convinced to accept the toy, but he didn't seem overly sure of the thing. "What if the ball hits me?"

"It might," Lord Jonquil said. "But it doesn't truly hurt."

"I don't want to get hit." He shoved the bilboquet back into his host's hands, then folded his arms in a posture that was likely meant to appear authoritative but came across far closer to petulant.

Lady Jonquil rose. "Adam, what do you know of Sir Isaac Newton?"

"He was a man of science, and he is not alive anymore."

The lady dipped her head in solemn acknowledgment. "Do you know that he developed a scientific theory that sought to explain the behavior of a toy?"

Interest entered little Adam's eyes. "A toy?"

Lady Jonquil nodded again.

Adam looked to Lord Jonquil.

"Julia is far more intelligent than I am," he said. "If you want the answer to a scientific question, you will need to inquire of her." There was not a bit of jesting in his tone and not even a hint of disapproval. Indeed, he spoke with absolute pride in his voice.

"Would you like to learn more about this toy?" Lady Jonquil asked Adam.

"Yes, please."

She opened the little chest of toys and diversions they'd brought out for Adam to enjoy. After a bit of digging, she pulled out three tops.

Adam eyed them, then her. "Tops?"

"Sir Isaac discovered a great many things about inertia and movement and gravitational forces. All these principles are part of what makes a top spin. There is much about the physical world that we do not truly understand. It is possible, in fact, that he will eventually be proven wrong in at least some of his theories. But he spent a great deal of time studying and pondering these things, and I do not think he is entirely in error."

Lady Jonquil lifted the hem of her robe à l'anglaise and sat on the floor. The wide gown pooled around her, stiffened at the sides by her panniers. She didn't wear as drastic a style as some ladies did. Then again, most ladies wouldn't sit on the floor to play with a child, regardless of what they were wearing.

"If the top is still, it falls over." She demonstrated for Adam.

Adam kneeled on the floor by her, concentrating on the toy. "You're supposed to spin it."

"You have used a top before." Lord Jonquil dropped onto the floor near them both.

"Of course I have." He sounded almost offended. His lack of familiarity with the other toys they'd suggested would make anyone wonder if he knew about toys at all.

"Centrifugal and centripetal forces are part of what makes things spin without falling over," Lady Jonquil said, setting the top to spinning with a quick and expert flick of her fingers. "We are still learning a great deal about what keeps the top spinning."

Adam watched, studying it. "What makes it stop?"

"Sir Isaac Newton wrote about a force he called gravity, which pulls all things toward the earth. It is believed the top falls on account of gravity," Lady Jonquil said.

"Why doesn't gravity knock it over while it's spinning?"

Lord Jonquil set another top awhirl. "Centripetal and centrifugal force."

With a firm nod, Adam declared, "This toy has a purpose. It makes cenpritipal and centrifipal force."

Neither Lord nor Lady Jonquil corrected his mispronunciations. Robbie breathed a sigh of relief. They had made progress with the frightened little boy. If he thought they were laughing at him or thought low of him, he would close off again.

Lady Jonquil set the remaining top in front of him. "You can use this one."

He eyed it with misgiving. Lord Jonquil laid down on the floor next to Adam and spun his top, watching it whirl. Robbie didn't know if Lady Jonquil remained seated rather than lying down because her dress required it of her or because she wasn't quite as spontaneous as her husband. But the lady did continue playing with the top.

Adam nudged it a bit but didn't try to play with it. After a moment, he hopped up and rushed to where Robbie sat.

"Why aren't you playing, wee boy?" she asked.

In a worried whisper, he said, "I don't remember how."

"You've seen Lord and Lady Jonquil spin their tops. Mimic what they do. You'll catch the knack of it soon enough."

"I'll do it wrong, and then I'll look ridiculous." That word again.

"What if you take your top in the entryway, away from everyone, and practice a bit until you've sorted it?" Robbie suggested. "Then you'd not have onlookers while you set yourself to remembering the trick of it."

Confidence reentered his expression. He rushed back over to his abandoned top and scooped it up. Tucking the toy against his black wool frock coat, he rushed from the room.

Lord and Lady Jonquil exchanged a series of looks, the sort that made up an unspoken conversation. Robbie had known a few couples with that kind of connection. She'd always wondered what that would be like. If servants were able to marry, she might've found that long ago. She didn't want to entirely abandon hope of it someday but didn't see how it was possible. She hadn't enough saved for living on if she lost her position.

She liked her job, and she felt she'd done some good in the lives of her little charges. There was satisfaction in that.

"I hope we didn't upset him," Lady Jonquil said to Robbie. "We were so certain he wouldn't have had toys to play with in his Harrow-adjacent boardinghouse. We thought he'd enjoy playing with them again."

"He frets over being seen as an object of pity," Robbie said. "He's received a crushing amount of it in his short life."

The duchess, Adam's mother, seemed to feel nothing but pity for her child. Visitors to Falstone Castle had often responded to the scarred state of his face with a suffocating version of sympathy.

"He thinks he has to play expertly with toys or we will pity him?" Lord Jonquil asked, still lying on his stomach and spinning his top. Robbie suspected he truly enjoyed games and lighthearted diversions. And yet he gave no impression of flightiness or immaturity or simpleness.

"He fears what is unfamiliar and unexpected. He fears he'll nae be good enough and will disappoint people."

"Oh, the sweet boy." Lady Jonquil looked in the direction of the doorway through which Adam had passed. "We simply must convince him he needn't fret over any of those things while he's here."

"He's in an unfamiliar place, with people he doesn't know well." Robbie sighed. "It won't be an easy feat getting that wee'un to be at ease with all that."

Lord Jonquil met her eye. "We've a builder here just now, putting in a walled garden. That's another stranger. And the back lawn will be torn up in places, and I have the strong impression Adam is not overly fond of chaos."

"I suspect the boy will give both the area of construction and your builder a wide berth."

"Mr. Simpkin seems a single-minded fellow," Lord Jonquil said. "He'll likely be too focused on his work to take much note of our little duke."

Robbie hoped that proved true. She'd have something to say on the matter if this stranger made her Adam unhappy.

Chapter Four

Howard knew he was good at what he did. But three days into his job at Brier Hill, he was having to pretend more confidence than he felt. He'd not been able to locate stone that matched the existing walls. He'd found local workers to help dig the footings, but only one of the four had any experience building a stone wall. He'd told Lord Jonquil he could complete this job in three weeks. The thought of having to tell his most important patron that he needed more time sat heavy on his mind.

He could not fail. This was an opportunity from heaven itself, one he was not likely to see again.

The sun sat high in the midday sky as he walked the length of the footing for the eastern wall. The men he had hired were doing a good job. The width was correct. The depth was correct. The workmen had kept their trench straight and sure. It would be completed by day's end. Delaying explaining about the stone to Lord Jonquil would only risk putting the project further behind schedule. Howard would simply have to do it.

The gentleman himself stepped out onto the back lawn not long after Howard determined his need to speak with him. The man dressed quite fashionably in silks and laces and buckled shoes, but he didn't give the impression of frivolity. There was a steadiness to the gentleman that gave Howard a small degree of reassurance.

Popping his hat into his hands, Howard approached.

"How progresses the work?" Lord Jonquil asked.

"Well. Well." Howard maintained his businesslike demeanor despite the concern in the back of his mind. "These local men are hard workers. They are digging a fine footing. I am needing to talk to you about something though."

Lord Jonquil must have heard the uncertainty in his voice. His gaze narrowed a little. "What is it?"

"I've inquired at all the local quarries, and not a one has stone that matches your existing walls. I can look farther afield, but it will slow the project and add to the cost." He watched his patron for signs of displeasure. What he saw was pondering. "I'll take whatever approach you'd like, my lord."

"If these walls were built of different stone, would the effect be an unpleasant one?"

Howard shrugged. "It'd depend on how different the stone was. Some would look odd together. Some would look complementary."

"Do any of these local quarries have stone that would be well-suited to the project?"

A bit of hope bubbled. If Lord Jonquil was open to the idea of a different type of stone, one that could be obtained in the area, that would speed up the work. Howard would not be forced to push back the completion date. "There's a quarry not far outside Hexham that has stone that would look nice."

"You're certain?" Lord Jonquil pressed.

This was firmer footing for Howard. He nodded. "I've used their stone before. Good quality, reasonable price. The color'd be a fine complement to what you have already. I haven't the least doubt."

"Then, I think we have a solution."

Howard popped his hat back onto his head, feeling a little less worried. It wasn't the only bridge that needed to be crossed, but it put him on the right path. He'd see that the footings were completed, then ride out to the quarry to arrange for the stone to be carted to Brier Hill.

Lord Jonquil wandered over to the workers. Howard held his breath for a moment; would His Lordship interrupt their work? He needn't have worried. The gentleman simply walked along the edge of the footing trench, looking on silently. His eyes scanned the area that would be the garden, the mountains in the background, the expanse of lawn around them. Howard hoped he was pleasantly picturing the space after the work was done.

He needed to make certain there were no more bumps, no more difficulties he needed to bring to Lord Jonquil. The gentleman had been understanding and reasonable, but even the most patient people remembered frustrations. Howard wanted his patron's praise of his work to be wholehearted.

Not far from the house, the young duke and the woman Howard assumed was the boy's governess stepped out onto the lawn. They'd not made a turn about the grounds in the three days since he had spotted them across the way. He assumed they had found other places to undertake their exercise. If they meant to make a habit of traversing this area, he needed to tell her a thing or two.

He wasn't merely worried about the boy causing problems with the work, though he *was* worried about that—there was also danger in little ones hanging about a worksite. The footing was deep and the child might fall in. Once the stones arrived, there was risk of being crushed. The woman looking after him needed to be careful.

He tossed back to his workers, "Keep at it. I'll rejoin you in a minute." Howard crossed the lawn toward the governess and her charge.

They caught sight of him as he approached, and neither one looked overly pleased. The governess was likely only a bit younger than his almost forty years. She wore her brown hair pulled up in a tidy but simple knot. Her clothes were, as he'd noticed the first time he'd seen her, those of the uncomplicated fashion of a servant. Being closer now than he'd been in past encounters, he could see that, even dressed and coiffed as modestly as she was, the duke's governess was rather striking. Her brown eyes were sharp and expressive. Her features were something more than merely pleasing; they were intriguing. Now, however, was not the time for mental wanderings on the topic of the woman's beauty.

Howard turned toward the little duke. He had met a few boys the same age as this one, but he had never seen one look so fearsome. The young duke wore a black frock coat over a gray-striped waistcoat with black breeches and black shoes. Only the white of his shirt and stockings broke up the somberness of his attire. The boy was, Howard knew, in mourning, but his appearance added an air of harshness more than of grief.

Howard dipped his head in deference to the boy's rank. "Your Grace, I need a word with your governess."

"She's not my governess." He spoke in fully imperious tones. No matter that he was just a little thing, Howard found himself taking a step back and feeling the urge to apologize.

"I am the nursemaid," the woman said. A Scotswoman, from the sound of her voice. That she was a nursemaid was a stroke of luck. Governesses could be full of their own importance; a nursemaid would be easier to reason with.

To the duke, he said, "Will you grant us a moment?"

With a twitch of his head so tiny as to put a fellow firmly in his place, the boy stepped away and returned to the house.

"A child needs fresh air and exercise," the nursemaid said. "I do nae appreciate you preventing His Grace from obtaining his."

Howard hadn't been expecting a scolding. This might not be as easy as he'd hoped.

"I only needed to drop a word of warning in your ear," he said.

"Oh, you do, do you?" She ruffled up.

He was making a bad beginning.

"We are undertaking a build just now, Mrs. . . ." He waited for her to fill in the missing name.

"Miss MacGregor."

Miss. Of courses she would be *Miss* MacGregor. Servants weren't generally permitted to marry and retain their positions. His thoughts were not so ordered and clear as he'd have hoped. Too much was spinning in his mind. "Miss MacGregor, you simply can't let His Grace run wild about the grounds."

Her laugh emerged as a snort.

"Why do you find that funny?" He'd not at all expected her to be amused.

She crossed her arms and cocked her head. "Have you ever known a duke to run wild anywhere?"

"I've never known a duke to be a small child, but I have known plenty enough small children, and running wild is what they do."

"Not this one." She tipped her chin up at a defiant angle. Quite sure of herself, wasn't she?

"This project's important to His Lordship," Howard said. "He'll be none too pleased if your charge wreaks havoc."

"*My charge* is important to Lord and Lady Jonquil. They'll be none too pleased if you cause him any distress."

"And none too pleased with you if the little duke gets himself hurt fussing around a building site."

"He doesn't fuss."

The woman was impossible. He was trying to caution her, and she would hear none of it. Accidents at building sites had killed people. He knew that all too well.

"I'll be keeping a weather eye out for that little duke," he said.

Her nostrils flared. "Are you issuing a warning?"

"Someone needs to save that child from himself, and it's clearly not going to be you."

Feeling more frustrated than when he'd first approached the woman, Howard spun around and marched away. The most important job he'd ever had, and now he not only had to overcome obstacles of stones and local workers but also the added difficulty of a little boy and his inattentive nursemaid.

Chapter Five

"I don't understand the purpose of this." Adam watched Lord Jonquil with tremendous confusion. The gentleman had suggested they walk up a mountain. He couldn't imagine why.

"Fresh air and exercise are good for a person," Lord Jonquil said. "And if one can obtain those things while doing something enjoyable, all the better."

That didn't sound right at all. "Walking up a mountain does not sound enjoyable."

"I can assure you," Lord Jonquil said, "it is tremendous fun."

Adam looked to Lady Jonquil, not trusting her husband's explanation. "I don't know anyone who walks up mountains."

"I do," she said.

Adam shook his head. "Other than him." He motioned to Lord Jonquil.

"We have five very good friends, all respected and proper gentlemen, and every one of them walks up our mountain whenever they're visiting. And I often go up with Lord Jonquil."

He hadn't expected that. "You do?"

She nodded.

"Do you enjoy it?"

She nodded again.

Perhaps people *did* enjoy the undertaking, but Adam wasn't entirely certain it was safe. "Do people fall off mountains when they walk on them?" He made certain to ask the question without a single tremor in his voice. He was cautious, but he didn't want them to think he was a coward.

"I would not for a moment suggest you go up that mountain if I thought you would be in the least danger." Lady Jonquil had a way of looking at him that made his mind calm and his heart warm. He almost never felt that way.

Adam glanced ever so quickly at Lord Jonquil, then stepped up very close to where Lady Jonquil sat and stood directly in front of her. She leaned a bit forward.

He whispered, "I've never walked on a mountain before. What if I'm rubbish at it?"

She took his hands. Hers were so soft. Were all ladies' hands soft?

"The first time I ever walked on a mountain was with him." She dipped her head toward Lord Jonquil. "And it was on this same mountain. I'm certain I *was* rubbish at it, but he didn't mind in the least. He loves being on that mountain, and he is excessively fond of company. He won't mind if you walk slowly or uncertainly; he'll simply be happy to be with you in a place he enjoys."

"No one is ever happy to be with *me*."

"Nurse Robbie loves to be with you," Lady Jonquil said. "And so do I."

The confusion in his mind pushed his brows and lips down. Sometimes people didn't make any sense. "Because I'm a duke?"

"Because you are *you*." She squeezed his hands, but not tight, not so they hurt.

He shook his head. "You say strange things."

"Someday, Adam, you will believe me." She released his hands and, taking light hold of his arms, turned him about.

Nurse Robbie stood right beside him, holding his coat. "I've asked Lord Jonquil about your jaunt today. He says you'll be safe during your adventure."

"Dukes don't have 'adventures.'" Adam was quite certain of that.

"Dukes can have all the adventures they wish for." She slipped one sleeve over his arm. "That is one of the advantages." She slipped on the other one.

"Do dukes have to go to school?" he asked.

She nodded. "When they are children, aye."

He didn't like that answer, but it wasn't a surprise.

"You could go up the mountain with us," he said. Nurse Robbie always looked after him.

But she shook her head. "This is a journey you need to take without me."

"I don't like taking journeys without you." He pushed down the lump in his throat. He'd cried when he'd left Falstone Castle to live near Harrow. Nurse Robbie hadn't come with him. He didn't like when she wasn't with him.

She buttoned the front of his coat. It was black, like all his clothes. He used to wear other colors, but a person had to wear black after someone in their family died. He wasn't certain why, but he had thought about it. He suspected it was important for people to know when someone was sad about people dying.

"You'll not be gone long, wee boy. And you'll be looked after."

He wasn't certain of that. "What if he forgets me and leaves me on that mountain?"

She gave him a doubtful look.

He returned it. "Mother forgets me all the time."

"Do you think, for even a moment, wee'un, that Lady Jonquil would let you be left up there?"

He looked around Nurse Robbie at the lady in question. She smiled. Her eyes were soft and kind.

Lord Jonquil hunched down next to Adam. "I've never, ever left anyone on any mountain. It is one of my unbreakable rules. Another is that I always bring food." He held up a knapsack and wiggled his eyebrows.

The silliness of his expression made a smile bubble inside Adam's ribs. He kept it tucked there; dukes weren't supposed to be silly.

"Another of my rules," Lord Jonquil said, "is that I never force anyone to do anything or go anywhere if he or she does not wish to. The decision is entirely yours, Adam."

Nurse Robbie didn't think he was in danger going onto the mountain. Lady Jonquil wanted him to go. And Lord Jonquil was very funny. Maybe a walk on the mountain wouldn't be terrible.

He could at least try. That would be a very brave thing. Dukes ought to be brave. He gave a nod to Lord Jonquil.

"Excellent." Lord Jonquil stood once more. He offered a formal bow to Nurse Robbie and to his wife. "We will now embark on our journey. Our apologies in advance for the overwhelming boredom you will experience without us."

Even Nurse Robbie laughed. She didn't do that often. The question of why weighed on Adam's mind as he and Lord Jonquil stepped from the house. Lord Jonquil whistled for his dog, Pooka, who rushed over immediately. Adam kept a safe distance. The dog wasn't large, but Adam had learned during his years at Falstone Castle that even small dogs could be ferocious.

He and Lord Jonquil rode in a pony cart away from Brier Hill and out to the mountain they meant to walk up. Adam only half noted the things they passed as the cart journeyed along. His mind was pulled between uncertainty over the dog and his worries about Nurse Robbie not laughing very often. Was she unhappy? People at Falstone Castle often were. He didn't want her to be unhappy. And he worried also about the fact that she didn't want to go on the mountain with him. Nurse Robbie had always liked being with him before. Had that changed?

Why was it grown people were so difficult to understand?

The cart came to a stop. Adam made himself pay more attention as he climbed down, not wanting to fall before they had even begun their walk on the mountain. Lord Jonquil gave the coachman who had driven them instructions on when to return, then the pony cart pulled away.

Lord Jonquil was watching Adam. Pooka was on a lead and tugging toward the mountain. Both the dog and the walk ahead of them worried Adam more than a little.

Dukes are meant to be confident. Adam's father had told him that. He wanted to be a good duke, so he firmed his shoulders and made his face very serious. "It would not do to waste time." He'd heard his father say that.

The path they walked on was not unlike most country footpaths. It wasn't terribly steep. There weren't a great deal of trees, though there were some. Adam's favorite part was that Pooka kept a whole lead-length ahead of them.

"Did you know I was your age when I first ventured up this mountain?" Lord Jonquil asked.

"Did you live here when you were little?"

"Sometimes. My grandfather was ill, so we lived at his house in Nottinghamshire most of the year."

"Did he die?"

"He did."

Adam tugged his hat a little lower on his head, not wanting to look up at Lord Jonquil. "My father died."

"There's sadness in the heart when a person dies." Lord Jonquil didn't tell him to stop being sad; people were forever telling him that. Maybe he understood about people dying and feeling sad about it. "Lady Jonquil's sister died when she was your age. Her mother died not long after that. I remember how sad her heart was."

"She doesn't seem sad." Maybe the sadness got better with time.

"She is happy to have you visiting," Lord Jonquil said. "She told me that, when she met you at Falstone Castle, you asked about her hair but you didn't say it was ugly. People used to say her hair was ugly when she was younger, and she didn't like that."

"The boys at the boardinghouse used to call me ugly, on account of my scars." He set his hands in his coat pockets. "But Jeb, at Falstone Castle, taught me how to fight. So when they said that, I trounced them. No one calls me ugly anymore."

"You are likely one of the youngest boys there. Can you really bash the older boys?"

Adam nodded, a surge of pride filling him. He even looked up at Lord Jonquil again.

"Do you have any friends at school? Boys you enjoy spending time with?"

"Dukes don't need people. My father taught me that."

"I predict, Adam, that someday you will have a friend, and you will be glad you do."

That was ridiculous. "Who would want to be my friend?"

"Any highwayman with ambition."

What a strange thing to say. Adam studied him. "What do you mean?"

"Land pirates need associates who are good with their fives." Lord Jonquil assumed a fighting stance, fists at the ready.

Adam understood now. "You're being silly."

"Nothing of the sort. Why, you'd be invaluable in a criminal enterprise. You can fight. You will soon be an expert at mountaineering. You have a forest, so you are likely *very* good at hiding in trees. And you have a castle, which means you likely have a dungeon."

Excitement pulled at his breath. "I have a gibbet."

"Excellent," Lord Jonquil said earnestly, but with a grin in his eyes.

Adam had to bite down on his lips to stop a laugh from bursting out of him.

They continued their upward walk, the trail they followed twisting about a little. It brought them to a spot where the ground was flat and no trees blocked the view of the valley around the mountain. Adam had never seen the world from up above it. He liked it.

Lord Jonquil sat on the ground, his back against a large rock. Adam did what Lord Jonquil did, assuming that was the best thing. Pooka's lead was wrapped around a branch on a nearby bush, but the line was not so short that the dog couldn't still explore. Lord Jonquil reached into his knapsack and pulled out two paper-wrapped sandwiches.

"Eat your fill," Lord Jonquil said. "You'll work up more of an appetite mountaineering than you realize and will run short of vigor on the way down if you don't eat now."

Adam obeyed. "Have I done a good job of walking up the mountain?"

"An excellent job." Lord Jonquil's eyes slowly roved over the scene in front of them, the valley and the trees around. "If you find you enjoy walking on mountains, we can jaunt over to Long Crag. That's another favorite of mine. A bit of a journey to get there but makes for a fine day's expedition."

"It's nice up here," Adam said. "It's really quiet."

"Sometimes quiet is nice, isn't it?" Lord Jonquil gave Pooka a scratch behind the ear as the dog wandered past.

Adam kept an eye on the dog, not entirely trusting it. "Nurse Robbie said the castle was quiet while I was away. Do you think she was glad I was gone?"

"I'd wager she missed you terribly."

"They had Christmas without me. I was at school."

That seemed to surprise him. "Your mother didn't wait to send you?"

Adam shook his head. "I was the only boy at the boardinghouse at Christmas. It was lonely." He hadn't told anyone that. Somehow, he didn't mind Lord Jonquil knowing.

"Then the other boys came back, and you likely weren't lonely enough." Lord Jonquil gave him a knowing look. Adam hadn't thought of it before, but Lord Jonquil would have gone to school when he was a boy. He'd know how miserable it was.

"I didn't like having Christmas there," Adam said.

"Too bad you haven't thrown your hat in with the highwaymen after all," Lord Jonquil said. "They likely have raucous Christmas festivities."

Adam tried to imagine highwaymen celebrating Christmas. It was a silly idea, but he couldn't push it out of his mind. Try as he might, he also couldn't stop himself from smiling. "What do highwaymen do at Christmastime?" He wondered out loud.

Lord Jonquil hopped up. He pulled off his coat and set it on a nearby branch. "Highwaymen always look a shambles."

He mussed his hair with his hands, pulling strands of it out of the ribbon that held it back. Pooka jumped about, apparently thinking they were playing a game of some sort. Lord Jonquil untied his cravat and shook it loose. He then tied it around his waist like a sash. He put one foot up on the rock he'd been leaning against and popped his fists onto his hips. He looked off into the distance with a very serious expression. Pooka barked at him, but in a sound that was more excited than angry. Adam didn't know dogs could bark in more than one way.

"We are highwaymen, Adam. At Christmastime, we have to steal things."

"Maybe highwaymen take a holiday from stealing at Christmastime."

Though Lord Jonquil didn't change his pose, he looked at Adam out of the side of his eye. "What do you suppose they do instead?"

Adam scrambled to his feet. He pulled off his coat as well. He mussed his hair, most of it already falling out of the string Nurse Robbie had tied it back with. He didn't have a cravat for making a sash, but he thought he looked the part well enough. He popped his fists onto his hips as well. "Instead of *taking* things from people, we should *give* things to people."

"Excellent." Lord Jonquil made his voice boom with importance.

"Excellent." Adam did his best to copy the sound.

Pooka barked again.

They spent a while longer on the mountain, eating their sandwiches and making up silly things for highwaymen to do at Christmastime. Lord Jonquil told Adam about some of the things he had done when he was a little boy and about his friend, Stanley, who had always wanted to have adventures.

Best of all, he told Adam that he liked spending time with him. No one ever seemed to. But he now knew four people who did: Lord Jonquil, Lady Jonquil, Jeb at the castle, and Nurse Robbie.

He would miss Lord and Lady Jonquil when he left Brier Hill. And he wouldn't see Jeb much now that he had to go to school at the boardinghouse.

But at least he had Nurse Robbie. He would always have Nurse Robbie.

Chapter Six

"WE NEED TO HOLD A Christmas celebration." Lord Jonquil waved Robbie into the book room after she put Adam to bed that night and made the pronouncement without preamble.

"A Christmas celebration?" she repeated, confused.

He nodded. "Apparently, he was sent away to Harrow just before Christmas."

"Aye. 'Twas a shame, that. I did try to convince his mother to let him remain." Robbie preferred to avoid speaking ill of the lady who now had such control over her employment, but that had been an unkind thing to do to her son.

"He spoke of it while we were on the mountain," Lord Jonquil said. "I think he would enjoy the chance to have the Christmas he missed."

Robbie looked to Lady Jonquil, who sat on a nearby sofa, listening intently. The lady sat with a hand laid gently on her middle, a position she assumed often. Though Robbie'd not been told as much directly, she suspected Lord and Lady Jonquil would be parents before the year's end.

"I think it would be wonderful," Lady Jonquil said, "but we defer to you. Adam is better known to you, as are the Christmas traditions at Falstone Castle."

"I'm afraid there weren't many," Robbie said. "When the old duke was alive, he and Adam would drink wassail and exchange little gifts. The servants put up greenery on Christmas Eve. Adam and his father would sing Christmas hymns. It was a quiet evening, always only the two of them. I'd wager that's what he misses most: being with his father."

"Do you think having a belated Christmas here would only add to his grief?" Lord Jonquil spoke as one who knew loss and one who had walked with others through their sorrows.

Robbie pondered the question for a long moment. "Were we to have this substitute Christmas at the castle, I think it'd be a difficult thing for him. He'd be faced over and over again with his father's absence."

A surprisingly charitable thought entered Robbie's mind: maybe the duchess had sent Adam away thinking it'd save him from the stark reality of Christmas at home without his father.

"Being here, where everything's new," Robbie added, "would lessen that association, I think. He'd nae be thinking of how he'd once done this with his father. Might be a healing thing for the wee boy."

"And we could always choose some traditions that were different from what he's known," Lady Jonquil said. "Then it would feel like Christmas but not like a Christmas focused on his loss."

"And"—Lord Jonquil's expression turned immediately mischievous—"we should give some thought to making our celebration a highwayman's Christmas."

Lady Jonquil looked as confused as Robbie felt.

"While we were on the mountain," Lord Jonquil explained, "we had such a laugh at the idea of highwaymen during the holy season. They would, we decided, spend Christmas giving people things instead of stealing from them. He thought the idea was an utter lark."

"Did he truly laugh?" Robbie asked.

Lord Jonquil nodded, quite as if it weren't a complete oddity. Adam never laughed. He seldom smiled. What magic were these two working on the solemn and grieving little boy?

"We should ask Mr. Simpkin if he would help us create some Christmas greenery," Lady Jonquil said. "He has such a lovely eye for plants and such. He would do a wonderful job, I'm certain." She looked to her husband. "He would help us, don't you think?"

"No," Robbie said, almost without thinking.

That brought both their eyes to her, surprise written on their faces.

"He grumped and groused about Adam being here," Robbie said. "Warned me against the child getting in his way. Gave me a dressing down, he did, as if I were neglecting my duties."

"That doesn't sound like him." Lord Jonquil looked more confused than doubtful.

"Bring up with him the matter of a little boy being on the estate," Robbie said. "It'll sound like him, sure enough."

Lady Jonquil rose. "I will go speak with him." On that declaration, she glided regally from the room.

Lord Jonquil grinned as he watched her leave. "We should likely pray for Simpkin."

"I think your wife might be a warrior." Robbie liked that the lady was wielding that fire on behalf of her beloved Adam.

"She loves that little duke." Lord Jonquil turned back to Robbie. "I'm grateful to you for bringing him. I'm certain it was more of an inconvenience than you've let on."

Robbie shook her head. "If you've lightened him enough for that heavy-hearted laddie to laugh, every effort will've been well worth making."

"And if Simpkin is willing to help us create this odd and magical Christmas we are plotting, would it be worth the effort of working with him?"

She held herself firmly and with determination. "I'd work with the devil himself if it brought my Adam joy. He deserves it more than any little boy I've known, and he's had less of it than even you can imagine."

Adam sat beside Lady Jonquil on the rattan furniture on the terrace at the back of the house. She had found him attempting to read Lord Jonquil's copy of the *Times* and had, through some miracle, convinced the boy to sit with her and read *The History of Little Goody Two-Shoes* instead. The book was far more fitting for a boy of eight. Seeing him focused and content, Robbie took advantage of the opportunity to step out onto the lawn and go for a bit of a walk.

She loved Adam, and she was grateful to still be in his life, caring for him and looking after him. But her mind remained heavy. The old duke's passing had prevented her from losing her position at the new year, but she knew even the neglectfulness of the duchess wouldn't allow her to remain Adam's nursemaid much longer.

The Duchess of Kielder would, she was certain, provide her with adequate references. Robbie would have no difficulty finding a new position, but she'd little enthusiasm for it. Was she simply so attached to Adam? So worried for him? Or had she grown weary of being a nursemaid? She wasn't likely to find work as anything else.

"Miss MacGregor?"

She stopped abruptly at the unexpected interruption to her ponderings. Mr. Simpkin stood in front of her, his expression as uninviting as ever.

"His Grace has caused you no difficulties," Robbie immediately asserted. "You cannot have any honest complaints against him, can you, now?"

To her surprise . . . *he* looked surprised. "I didn't stop you to complain."

"You've been seized by some mind-softening fever, then?"

He didn't seem to know whether to be offended or amused. Good. If the man could be a bit upended, he might not have the wherewithal to cause her grief.

"What *was* your purpose in stopping me?"

"Lady Jonquil asked me to gather some greenery for the Christmas celebration."

She folded her arms fiercely. "And what has that to do with me?"

"Don't ruffle up, woman. I've not come to you with an argument." He shook his head. "I don't know what sort of boughs and garlands are usually hung at that drafty old castle where you and your little duke live. As this is meant to be a celebration for him, I thought I'd do best to find out."

That was actually a thoughtful reason to have interrupted her. Not at all what she'd expected. "I'll nae necessarily have the accurate names for them," she said.

Mr. Simpkin shrugged. "Describe 'em. It's the best way."

"Garlands of evergreen are placed on mantels and windowsills. Evergreen wreaths are hung on doors. The servants usually made kissing boughs, but those were only ever hung in the belowstairs; the old duke did nae care for that tradition. So our wee duke would nae necessarily be familiar with them."

"There are likely some evergreens up a bit, toward the mountain. Nearer by, we could probably find other bits of flora to fill in what's needed."

Robbie eyed him, unsure how he truly felt about the matter. "You're likely put out with the lot of us, pushing on you this distraction from the job you came here to do."

He shook his head. "I don't mind. Christmas was a special time of year when I was a child. It'll be a bit of a lark to celebrate it in the spring."

"And what of your building project?" Robbie asked.

"I'm waiting on supplies just now. I'd rather have something to do than be idle."

To her great surprise, she felt a kinship to the man just then. Nothing overly fond, but a bit of understanding.

"I'll see what I can find," he said as he made his way toward his odd traveling coach. Robbie brushed off the strange interaction and made her way back toward the terrace.

Adam abruptly stopped his reading and looked directly at her. "Why were you talking to him?"

Oh dear. They'd decided the Christmas celebration would be a surprise. She couldn't be full honest with Adam, but she also didn't care to lie. He struggled to trust people as it was; being deceitful would only add to that.

"He had a question about the gardens and plants at Falstone Castle."

Adam's expression hardened. "Why does he care about the castle?"

"It is a fine auld home. And the planted forest must be of interest to a man who makes his living creating gardens and landscapes."

"I don't like him asking so many questions." His little mouth pulled into a mighty frown. "And he shouldn't be bothering you."

"He wasn't, Adam."

"You didn't like when he talked to you last time."

He'd noticed that, had he?

"Well, he was friendlier this time."

Adam assumed the expression of fierce determination she was all too familiar with. "He'd better keep being friendly. I already don't like him."

That was not a reassuring evaluation. Adam didn't like a lot of people. He'd too vast a history of being hurt. And yet one ought never to be dismissive when a child felt an instant distrust of someone.

Perhaps it would be best if Robbie kept up the interactions with Mr. Simpkin as they prepared for the surprise festivities. She could keep an eye on him, just as he'd sworn to keep an eye on Adam.

Chapter Seven

To Robbie's surprise, Adam went on another adventure with Lord Jonquil. This time, he didn't need convincing. They weren't going up a mountain or doing anything else that the little boy might consider dangerous or unusual. They were going to take the pony cart to the nearby village of Alnbury and spend a jaunty afternoon larking about.

While Robbie knew the outing would afford her an opportunity to begin preparations for the surprise Christmas celebration, she also felt confident that Lord Jonquil genuinely enjoyed spending time with Adam. But did he realize how much the boy needed it? His father had been nearly all of Adam's little world. To have another gentleman make room for him and spend time with him would help the void left in his life by his father's death feel a little less like it was going to swallow him.

Mr. Simpkin stood in the entryway, hat in his hands, when Robbie arrived there. His nod of acknowledgment was not gushing with friendliness, but neither was it insulting. The plan for the afternoon was for Robbie and Lady Jonquil to join him in the pony cart and discover what greenery was available for making their Christmas decorations.

"Has your stone still not arrived?" she asked. She couldn't imagine he would have agreed to this outing otherwise.

"It has not." His brows pulled together. "I don't usually have this much trouble."

"Fortunately, you've a bit of distraction at hand."

He smiled a little. It was a nice change in him. "I do like evergreens."

"Is there a variety of tree you don't like?" she asked.

His light smile remained. "I can't say there is."

Lady Jonquil stepped into the entryway. She looked pale. Worryingly so.

"Are you unwell, my lady?" Robbie asked.

"I confess I am feeling a little poorly." Her hand pressed momentarily to her middle. "That hasn't happened as often of late."

Ah. "A lady I worked for a few years back also felt a bit poorly when she was—well . . ."

Lady Jonquil saved her the trouble of finding the right level of delicacy and simply nodded her understanding.

"She found some relief from ginger tea," Robbie said. "That and a lie down would likely help tremendously."

Lady Jonquil pinched at her bottom lip. "I wouldn't disappoint Adam for all the world."

She had a good and generous heart.

"I'll make certain you have all the greenery you need," Mr. Simpkin said. "And I'll happily scout it out as well. You look after yourself, my lady."

That was an unexpected kindness.

"I can't ask you to do that," Lady Jonquil said, shaking her head. "We are pulling you from your work as it is. Requiring you to see to this errand on your own when it was not yours to begin with would be terribly unfair."

"I'm more than willing," he insisted.

"While I do appreciate that, I cannot countenance allowing it." Her expression turned determined even as her pallor increased. The poor lady would work herself into true illness if she did not take care. And yet her concern over burdening the garden builder might very well push her to it.

"I'm meaning to go with him," Robbie said. "Two will make the task faster. And you needn't worry that he's being left to carry a burden alone simply because you are unwell."

"Are you certain?" Lady Jonquil pressed.

Robbie nodded firmly. "We can make short work of the task. You, meanwhile, can rest until your husband is home."

The poor lady sighed a little. "I am exceptionally tired."

"Do rest, my lady," Mr. Simpkin said. "Miss MacGregor and I can manage this task."

With a nod, she agreed. She made her way toward the staircase and would, no doubt, retire to her bedchamber.

"You don't think her feeling unwell is a sign of trouble with her condition, do you?" Mr. Simpkin asked. "I'd hate for that to happen to so kindhearted a lady."

Robbie shook her head. "Many women feel poorly while awaiting an arrival. She still seems quite hale and hearty though. I ken she's simply a little worn down today."

"Then, I'm glad we can take this task off her mind."

"I'm glad of it myself."

It was an odd thing, having so friendly and agreeable a conversation with a man she'd only recently declared in need of watching. He was a confusion, and no denying.

"We'll not be gone long," he said, leading her to the waiting cart. "I believe we'll find a stand of evergreens not far up the road. And I've seen a few different types of trees between here and Alnbury. We could use branches from those as well."

They were quickly situated and on their way.

"Christmas must mean a whole heap to the little duke to be going to such trouble," Mr. Simpkin said as he led the horse down the road.

"Whether or not the holy season matters to him," Robbie said, feeling herself grow vexed on the instant, "that 'little duke' means a whole heap."

Mr. Simpkin shook his head. "I wasn't offering any insults, only an observation."

Robbie couldn't entirely sort him out. In some ways he very much reminded her of the late duke, who had a tendency to grumble. And yet there was an openness to him that'd been entirely lacking in Adam's father.

"Boughs and wreaths were specifically asked for, I recall," Mr. Simpkin said.

"Aye." Robbie nodded. "Those were always present during Christmas at Falstone Castle."

"Have you any objections to adding vases of flowers or trimmings made of flowers to our collection of evergreens?"

"I've not," she said. "And His Grace won't either."

"I'd like to create a few things that Lady Jonquil will be pleased with, even outside of this Christmas celebration." Mr. Simpkin guided the horse down a path leading in the direction of the nearby mountain. "And I know Lord Jonquil is fond of flowers. A great many early spring flowers have made their appearance. We can easily find hyacinths and tulips, and we have to include daffodils."

Robbie was confused. "Why is that?"

"A jonquil is a variety of daffodil," he said.

"Is it? I'd wager Lord Jonquil requested jonquils be planted in his garden."

A note of pondering entered his expression. "He didn't, actually. I wonder why that is."

"Perhaps he's nae thought of it," Robbie said. "A shame, that. Daffodils are fitting, given the family surname, and they're beautiful. They'd be lovely in any garden."

"I have a brilliant idea," Mr. Simpkin said, excitement touching his features. The eagerness softened his expression in a surprising way, and Robbie found she very much liked the sight of it. "If Lady Jonquil agrees, I could plant jonquil bulbs in the garden without telling her husband. Next spring, they'll bloom and, I'd wager, prove a very pleasant surprise."

It was, indeed, a brilliant idea. "I hope she agrees."

"I'd wager she will." Mr. Simpkin grinned. The man, grumpy and often off-putting, actually looked jovial. The way his face naturally slipped into the lines of a smile told her he smiled far more often than their earliest encounter had indicated.

"What else do we have at our disposal for decorating?" Robbie asked, eyeing the shrubs and trees and hedgerows they passed.

"Anything that grows wild and is blooming this time of year," he said. "Brier Hill hasn't a conservatory like some other fine houses have."

"Have you ever worked in a fine house?" Robbie asked.

He shook his head. "I come from generations of builders. It's all the Simpkins have ever done."

"Build gardens?"

"No. That's a twist I put on it myself." He pulled the cart over to the side of the road and hopped out. He came around to her side and handed her down. "Have you *always* worked in households?"

"Since I was ten years old."

They walked a pace off the road and among a stand of evergreens. Mr. Simpkin eyed the trees, but she didn't think he was ignoring her.

"I worked as a 'tween-stairs maid," she continued, "and then a chambermaid. I was fortunate to be given a chance to work as a nursery maid when I was seventeen. I found I'd a talent for it. I like working with children more than with their parents."

She glanced at him quickly, wondering if he would criticize her for that. Not everyone abided servants speaking ill of those they worked for. But he was occupied with examining branches and evergreen needles and didn't seem the least disapproving of her admission.

"How long have you been a nursemaid to the little duke?" he asked.

"All his life. I was hired at the time of his mother's confinement. I've been at Falstone Castle all the years since."

He moved to the next tree. "And has he any brothers or sisters?"

"No, he doesn't. As his father recently passed away, there'll not be any others."

Mr. Simpkin met her eye. In his expression she saw undeniable compassion. "Enduring that loss so young is a heavy thing. Poor child."

"It's not been an easy few months," she said. "Lord and Lady Jonquil invited His Grace to bide here a few weeks. I suspect they felt the change of scenery would give him something of a respite from his grief."

"And what happens when he goes back? Eventually, grief catches up to a person."

"You speak as one who knows."

He returned his gaze to the trees, but there was no hiding the pain written on his face. "My father died not quite a year ago. The sorrow of it still catches me unsuspecting now and then."

Robbie's thoughts instantly fled back years and over miles. She hadn't seen or heard from her family in more than two decades. Her siblings were scattered all over the kingdom. She'd passed those years raising other people's children and safeguarding other people's families, yet she'd not even the smallest family connection to claim for herself.

"I suspect Lord Jonquil will be disappointed if we're not able to find any mistletoe," Mr. Simpkin said.

She didn't know if the abrupt change of topic was for her sake, her pensiveness having been noticed, or was simply a happy coincidence, but she was grateful for it. "Why is it you think that?"

"The master and mistress of Brier Hill are rather nauseatingly in love."

"I don't find it nauseating at all."

He sighed in a way that very nearly sounded like a growl. "Why is it you ruffle up at everything I say? I wasn't insulting Lord and Lady Jonquil or speaking ill of love. I was attempting to have a friendly conversation with you."

Why was it he set her back up so easily? Likely because they'd begun on a bad footing. Their very first conversation had been him warning her not to let Adam get in his way.

"I'd wager Lord Jonquil will nae be bothered since he likely means to kiss his wife either way." She attempted a conciliatory smile, hoping he recognized her attempt at a joke as the peace offering it was.

"And the little duke will likely be just as squeamish at the display whether the couple kisses of their own accord or at the behest of a plant," Mr. Simpkin said.

Robbie couldn't help a smile. How well she remembered many of her young charges over the years growing squirmy at just such a thing. She suspected they appreciated knowing their parents cared about each other, even if they'd no enjoyment for seeing a kiss between them.

She hadn't the first idea how Adam would respond to such a thing. While she wouldn't say his parents necessarily despised each other, they'd not been on friendly terms. That might be another benefit of this trip to Brier Hill: he'd see a happy marriage and experience a welcoming and peaceful home.

"These are pliant enough for making boughs and wreaths." Mr. Simpkin tugged on a branch. "How extensively decorated was Falstone Castle at Christmastime?"

"Only a wee bit," Robbie admitted.

Mr. Simpkin nodded. "I'll fetch an armful the day Lady Jonquil wishes to begin decorating."

"Along with wildflowers and such?"

He nodded. "I'm counting on the two of you to know how to pleasantly arrange it all. My expertise lies with planting the foliage, not crafting it into decorations. I'll simply try to find things that are pleasant and green and filled with life. That is what Christmas is, after all—a celebration of life during that time of year when the world slumbers. The leaves have fallen. The landscape is barren. And yet in the midst of that darkness comes this moment when life returns. Life and light and hope."

For a moment Robbie could hardly breathe. He'd spoken casually, quite as if he'd not just made a beautiful observation. It was an unguarded moment in which she saw a side of this man she'd not expected. This builder of walls and planter of flowers had a poet's heart.

"That is what we must make this celebration," she said. "Adam's known too much loss and darkness. He needs to feel hope."

"You likely think me strange for saying so," he said, "but that is why I do the job I do. There is life in nature. There is hope in the cycle of it. Planning a garden or an expansive lawn or a conservatory that will change with the seasons without going entirely barren brings people hope."

"Is that why you don't mind helping us with this even though it is pulling you away from your work?"

"I will confess it *is* interfering. But it seems to me this is part of what I've come here to do."

Robbie'd always had a healthy respect for the hand of fate. It had, she was full certain, brought Adam to this house, where he could feel wanted and peaceful. It had, apparently, also brought Mr. Simpkin so he could offer hope.

What remained to be answered, though, was why fate had brought *her* to Brier Hill.

Chapter Eight

Howard's excursion with Miss MacGregor the day before had offered a much-needed escape from the frustration of the job he'd come to Brier Hill to complete. His stone hadn't arrived. Most of his planting couldn't be done until the wall was complete. All the while time was ticking away.

But that brief afternoon jaunt and the amiable gab he'd shared with a woman who, at first meeting, had seemed rather more like a fishwife than a friendly sort had restored his spirits. He'd returned to his corner of the estate with more hope than he'd left with.

He set himself to the task of laying bricks for the garden beds, leastwise those nearest the existing walls. It was work he could accomplish while waiting for his stone.

He'd passed a morning and good portion of an afternoon when Miss MacGregor arrived.

"I've a spot of time on my hands," she said. "Can I do anything to help?"

"The soil in the beds here needs breaking up," he answered.

She gave a quick nod and fetched from among his tools a grubbing hoe—the exact right tool for the job. He watched her a minute as she worked. Poor technique could cause pain or injury.

He needn't have worried. She set to the work with expertise borne of experience.

"Why is it you're not looking after your little duke just now?" he asked, kneeling once more to continue his brickwork. "Is he napping?"

Miss MacGregor spoke as she worked. "He's too old now for napping, except on rare occasions. He's passing the afternoon with his host and hostess. They've asked him to help them decide what's most needed to turn one of the bedchambers into a nursery."

Howard doubted they actually needed the help of an eight-year-old. But he'd discovered in his interactions with them that they were compassionate and generous people. They had likely chosen to involve the little duke because they thought he would enjoy it. He likely needed to feel part of a family in some way. Howard was thirty-eight years old, but he still keenly felt the loss of his parents.

"Watching them with the duke," Miss MacGregor said, "I've not a spot of doubt they'll be fine parents, doting and caring in a way many of their station are nae."

There was no mistaking she was Scottish, and yet her manner of speaking wasn't so decidedly that of Scotland that he was left to wonder. He'd wager she'd lived quite some time on this side of the Scottish border.

"Perhaps Lord and Lady Jonquil will be looking for a nursemaid," he said. "Your charge is at the age where he is unlikely to have one much longer. Might be your coming here will offer you an opportunity to find a new position without too much difficulty."

She paused in her digging, her face taking on a very thoughtful expression. It seemed she hadn't considered the possibility of being hired on at Brier Hill. He couldn't tell, however, whether she was pleased with the prospect.

"They'd likely be right generous employers," she said as if talking to herself. "And they're young yet, so there might be more children, which'd give me some longevity in the position."

"You'll likely think me terribly nosy, but you don't sound overly enthusiastic about what seems to be a perfect situation."

She returned to her efforts at breaking up the soil. "Working here, for this family, would be ideal in many ways. But I confess I find myself wondering lately whether I want to spend another twenty years looking after other people's bairns."

"Are you not enjoying your work?"

"I've enjoyment in it. But that might owe more to my attachment to the young duke than to the job of nursemaid itself."

"Are you always as attached to your charges as you are to this one?" He leaned back on his feet and eyed her, ready for some kind of fighting response. He intended to head it off. "I wasn't criticizing, only observing that you very clearly care deeply for him. I've seen other children of the Quality with their nurses, and there's not ever been quite so much attachment between them as I see between you and this little duke."

"I've been fond of all the children I've tended, but none has needed me the way he does. None of them has been as alone as he is. Falstone Castle is very isolated. He's no neighbors, no little playmates."

"I can't imagine a childhood like that. I came from a large family and had a great many little friends in the village where we lived. I loved it."

A nostalgic smile touched Miss MacGregor's face, and the effect was lovely. She was pretty—he'd always thought so—but something about that particular smile made a person want to smile in return.

"My family was much the same in my earliest years," she said. "We'd quite a few children in the household. We worked hard, but we also enjoyed each other."

"You told me when we were scouting out evergreens that you've been in service since you were ten years old. Did all your family seek employment so young?"

"My father was injured in an accident and could nae work. My mother and my older siblings were already supporting the family, but it was no longer enough. All but the youngest two among us found positions. We were employed as servants in households and had to leave home. Last I heard from any of them, my mother told me the youngest had also left to find work. We're spread out across the kingdom. I'm not even certain where most of them are."

His heart ached at that. So many who didn't bear the weight of poverty dismissed its ability to touch every aspect of a life. "Did your earliest jobs take you away from Scotland?"

She nodded. "Aye. They've all taken me away from there."

"I'd wager your parents are in Scotland still. Have you traveled back to see them?"

"Nursemaids haven't that flexibility. We go wherever the children of the family are. If they are at home, we bide there. If they travel with their parents, we go as well. Our comings and goings aren't our own."

He nodded in understanding. "I travel constantly for my work, never staying in one place for long. My home is the traveling coach I converted into a house of sorts. I don't have a home village to return to or call my own."

"You told me your father died last year. Were you able to see him before he passed?"

"I was, thank the saints. I've more freedom in that respect than you do. I don't have roots anywhere, but I can travel."

"I'd enjoy traveling," she said. "I've heard about some bonnie areas of this kingdom, mostly from the books I read to Adam. His is a particularly curious mind. He is forever asking questions. When we read about a new place, he asks me what it looks and feels like and how it smells. I have to tell him I don't know. He usually grows frustrated and says he would nae want to know anyway."

"He's a little petulant, is he?"

"No, not truly." She didn't sound offended, for which he was grateful. "He's spent so much of his life being hurt and overlooked and left behind. When he suspects he's about to suffer a fresh blow or a new wave of pain, he closes himself off, shields himself with anger. I don't know how to help him with that." Her shoulders drooped a bit. "He has no constant but me now, and once his mother sorts out that he is really too old for a nursemaid, I'll be forced to leave him, just as everyone else has. I worry that the shield of anger he wields will be turned to armor and the tenderhearted little boy I know will disappear inside it."

Howard's heart was both touched and sad at the sorrow he heard in her voice. He crossed to where she stood, hoping she saw in him the friendly rapport he was trying to offer. "No matter where life might take you, he will benefit from having been loved by you. Over the years, when he wonders if people care about him, he'll remember that you did. He'll trust that you *do*. That will make a great difference."

"That's a shocking thing to hear you say, considering you once insisted I was neglecting him so severely that you were needing to look after him on my behalf."

He winced a bit as the dart hit its mark. "Heavens, I did say that. My only defense is that I was concerned."

"About him or about your job?"

"Both. I do not want to see the child hurt. I also don't want to see my livelihood disappear."

"That sounds very much like the conversations I've been having with myself lately." She sighed. "My employment at Falstone Castle cannot last forever. Staying in the area so I can keep an eye out for Adam would mean having no job and no income. But leaving entirely would cause him such pain."

"For two people who began their acquaintance quite at odds, we seem to have a great deal in common." He smiled, hoping to encourage her and lighten her thoughts a little.

She smiled back, and it did the oddest thing to his heart, setting it pounding against his ribs in a way clearly meant to get his attention. He, however, was quite adept at ignoring it.

"This is the flower bed where I mean to plant the jonquils as a surprise for His Lordship."

"Lady Jonquil agreed, then?" Miss MacGregor seemed genuinely pleased.

"The lady thought it as brilliant an idea as we do."

Miss MacGregor looked around. "The trench is where the wall will be built?"

"Aye." Though not Scottish himself, he'd heard that word often enough to be able to reproduce it just as the Scots would say it.

"And the gate'll be just there?" She pointed toward the gap in the trench.

"Aye."

"And what will lie between here and there?"

He took the grubbing hoe from her and leaned it against the existing wall. He guided her over to where the gate would be and positioned her and himself so that they were looking at what would soon be the walled garden. He explained to her what was planned, where the larger tree would be as well as the smaller shrubs, which were flower beds and what flowers would be in them. He walked with her along what would be the stone path. He pointed out the spot where benches would be placed, explaining that one would be in the shade and the other in the sun so visitors could choose between the two.

Miss MacGregor asked impressive questions. Once or twice she offered an alternate idea to what he had planned. She showed herself to have a fine eye for plants and landscapes. She knew trees and bushes and flowers more than he would've expected from one who'd passed more than twenty years of her life working inside homes.

"Are you certain you haven't secretly been filling the role of gardener somewhere?" he asked.

Her smile blossomed ever broader, and his heart pounded ever harder. "I do occasionally work on the grounds at Falstone Castle. The gardener there allows me to join him. I've found I like spending a bit of time out in nature. There's something nice about the feel of the earth in one's hands, and I've just as curious a disposition as Adam does. I've asked a great many questions of the gardener, likely driving the poor man mad. But I've learned a whole heap from him, and he now eagerly welcomes my assistance. I've a great deal more time on my hands with Adam away at school."

That surprised him. "I didn't realize the Quality sent their sons away to school so young."

"Very few do. He is, in fact, too young to truly begin his schooling. But there's a boardinghouse that sits just outside of Harrow School, where the underage boys who've been sent away are given some schooling and a place in which to live out the years until they're old enough to pass through the school gates and begin their *formal* education."

"Sounds rather like an orphanage."

Her eyes grew sad once more. "To hear Adam speak of it, the place *feels* that way as well."

"It's no wonder, then, that you are so eager to give him this Christmas celebration. This tiny duke needs a spot of happiness in his life."

"You called it hope. I cannot clear my mind of that word. More than anything, he needs hope. The more life pulls people away from him, the more he's sent away and left behind, the more he'll struggle to feel it."

"While he's here, he'll be surrounded by it."

"Thank you for helping," she said. "I know you didn't come here to throw a party for a wee boy. It speaks well of you that you don't begrudge him the time you're spending."

"And it speaks well of you that you've a love for shrubs and trees and nature."

"That *is* the sort of thing you'd praise in a person." The observation might have felt like a criticism before their last couple of encounters. He now saw it for the dry humor it was.

They set back to their work, he laying bricks and she turning over soil. Conversation between them was easy. He often hired on workers to help him, but the words passing between them were generally limited to discussions of the work and corrections of their efforts. He couldn't remember the last time he'd undertaken a job with someone he could easily gab with.

"What other plans do the lot of you have for this Christmas celebration?" he asked as the day went on.

"Lord and Lady Jonquil are planning to undertake some games. That was a tradition they had growing up. It turns out they were wee childhood friends; they've a shared history."

"Perhaps that's why they seem so deeply bonded." He began laying bricks for another bed. "Did your family have any Christmas traditions before all of you had to go your separate ways?"

"We'd bring in greenery to brighten the house. Mother'd make the finest meal we could afford. It was never anything truly fine, but she made what she could. We made little gifts for each other. It was quiet, but it was joyful."

"Sounds very much like mine from childhood. There's something to be said for simplicity."

"My father always said it's people that make Christmas special, nae things."

"That is very much the philosophy for this party you're planning. Your lonely little duke will be surrounded by people who care about him, and that will make the day special."

"I hope so."

Miss MacGregor stayed another hour, working tirelessly and chatting amiably. He accomplished every bit as much as he always did, but he enjoyed it far more. He liked working with someone who felt like a friend. How easily he could imagine himself having someone in his life he could work with and talk with.

He tried not to ponder too closely the fact that his mind had begun formulating a picture of that someone, and she had a fiery temper, the smile of an angel, and a lilt in her voice that spoke of a childhood spent in Scotland.

Chapter Nine

ADAM TALKED MORE THAN USUAL as he and Robbie rode in a pony cart to the nearby village the following day.

"Lord Jonquil and I came here two days ago," he said. "He showed me all the best shops. It's a small village, but it still has shops."

"Even small villages have shops," she told him.

"I didn't know that." The poor boy had been to so few places; it was no wonder he understood so little about the world. "Lord Jonquil knows that. He knows a lot of important things."

Important things. Like villages having shops. Robbie hid her amusement. She'd learned from experience that Adam was sensitive about being laughed at. He didn't always understand the difference between someone finding enjoyment in what he'd said and someone mocking him. Lord Jonquil was a jovial person, who laughed often and frequently, but he was never unkind. That might help Adam come to understand the difference.

"What about Lady Jonquil?" she asked. "Does she know a great many important things as well?"

"Oh yes. More even than Lord Jonquil. She reads a lot of books. She showed me her books in her book room. She doesn't read silly books either. She reads important ones about places all over the world and about mathematics and science. Lord Jonquil says she's the smartest person he's ever met. Did you know ladies can be clever?"

Again, Robbie tucked away her smile. "Oh, aye, I knew that."

"Lord Jonquil says we can walk on his mountain again. He says I'm getting very good at it. I didn't know I could be good at walking on mountains."

"When I was a wee girl, I lived in Scotland. We've very tall mountains there."

He looked up at her. "Did you ever walk on them?"

"I did nae."

He nodded slowly, contemplatively. "Maybe someday Lord Jonquil and I will go to Scotland and walk on those mountains."

"I suspect he would like that very much," Robbie said.

"Did you know Lord and Lady Jonquil will have a baby come to their house this year?"

"I did."

His dark brows pulled low in a look she knew well. He was worried about something. Again.

"Do you suppose when they have a baby of their own, they won't want me to come see them anymore?"

Life had taught him to anticipate abandonment. And even here, in a place where he was more lighthearted than he'd just about ever been and was being shown he was wanted, he'd already prepared himself to be forgotten.

"They do not strike me as the type of folks who forget someone they love."

He turned wide eyes up to her. In a tiny, hesitant voice he asked, "Do you think they love me?"

"My wee Adam, I've nae a doubt in the world that they love you."

He was very quiet after that. She couldn't tell whether he was reassured by her words. More than anything, he looked confused.

They reached the outer edges of Alnbury. The coachman who'd driven them there dropped them on the high street before making his way to the pub, where he meant to pass the time before they were ready to return.

Robbie held her hand out to Adam, but he didn't take it. She was forever having to remind herself about that change in him. He'd returned from Harrow more distant in so many ways.

As they walked past shops, Adam told her about each and every thing they saw. Most of his explanations included Lord Jonquil's opinion on the various items. How Robbie hoped she was right about His Lordship. He'd quickly taken on the roles of older brother, uncle, and father somehow all rolled up into one. If he did forget about Adam after his own family began to grow, it'd be yet another devastating blow to this child who had already endured too many.

They'd only just stepped out of the confectionery shop, each enjoying a peppermint stick, when their paths crossed with Mr. Simpkin. For reasons Robbie couldn't fully explain, seeing him made her blush. She'd nothing to be embarrassed about. They'd passed a pleasant couple of hours working in the garden the day before. Their conversation had occasionally touched on more personal topics but nothing inappropriate or worthy of regret. The time they spent looking for trees from which to make Christmas decorations had been quite pleasant. Yet seeing him made her insides squirm about the same way they had when she'd worked for a family in Cumberland who'd had a stablehand she'd found particularly handsome. The same way they had when she was sixteen and working as a chambermaid in Derbyshire and one of the local lads had made sheep's eyes at her. She understood the reaction for what it was—her heart growing a wee bit partial to a handsome man who'd shown himself to be good company—but she was hardly in a position to let those feelings grow, so she pushed them down and summoned her best manners.

Mr. Simpkin bowed to Adam, as was expected, for he, though a little boy, held one of the highest ranks in all the land. Only the royal family ranked above a duke. And the Duke of Kielder was one of the oldest and most respected titles in the kingdom. Adam, she didn't doubt, would bring even more prestige to it as he grew. He was clever and determined. He held his father's legacy in such esteem that she couldn't imagine him ever allowing the title his beloved father had held to be anything but revered. And, if he was fortunate enough to retain the presence of Lord Jonquil in his life, he would have someone to guide him toward being a peer, in the best possible way.

But, for now, he was a child, one adults were required to bow to but none were required to love.

Adam watched Mr. Simpkin with obvious displeasure. Robbie had not yet sorted the reason for that. Her opinion of him was improving, not deteriorating. Why, then, was Adam not having the same experience? No sooner had the thought entered her mind than she realized the difficulty: he'd not spent time with Mr. Simpkin.

"What brings you to the village, Miss MacGregor?" Mr. Simpkin asked.

"His Grace wished to show me around."

Mr. Simpkin dipped his head to Adam once more. "Very thoughtful of you, Your Grace."

Adam didn't answer but watched Mr. Simpkin with an unwavering gaze. There was a hardness to it that spoke not of petulance but of fierceness. His was an expression that told the recipient that his respect was not easily earned but was worth obtaining. How, in heaven's name, had he learned the trick of that in the short time he'd been away at school? He was eight years old; he ought not be hardened yet.

"What has brought *you* to the village?" Robbie asked Mr. Simpkin.

"I came to see if word had arrived about the stone I'm waiting for."

"It's nae yet arrived?"

He shook his head. "It'll be another couple of days yet. I'll do all I can to work while I'm waiting. I'd not wish to waste Lord Jonquil's time."

Adam spoke for the first time since Mr. Simpkin's arrival. "Nurse Robbie helped you for two hours yesterday. I hope you did not waste her time either." Again, he managed not to sound like a little boy having a temper tantrum but very much like his late father had when issuing a directive. His was the same tone of authority, the same unwavering competence.

"Nurse Robbie was enormously helpful," Mr. Simpkin responded. "It seems she has learned a great deal from the gardener at Falstone Castle."

Adam's chin tipped at a proud angle. "We have a very good groundskeeper at the castle. My father chose him himself."

Mr. Simpkin nodded. "Your father was clearly a very wise man and a good steward of his estate."

Some of Adam's animosity slipped away. But only some. "Have you any other business in the village?" he asked.

"I do not," Mr. Simpkin said. "I do not wish to keep you from yours."

Were Adam anyone other than who he was, Robbie would have immediately invited Mr. Simpkin to stay. But, if one were being quite technical, she *had* to defer to Adam publicly. Child or not, he was a duke.

To Adam she said, "Would you mind if Mr. Simpkin joins us? If he remains, he can ride back with us in the pony cart. This will save some time and allow him to return to his work more quickly, which Lord and Lady Jonquil would nae doubt appreciate."

His mouth tightened in a tense line. She thought for a moment that he meant to refuse. He didn't, but neither did he offer any false declarations of pleasure. He simply gave one tiny nod and looked away.

She met Mr. Simpkin's eye and tried to offer a silent apology. He simply smiled and motioned for her to continue on her way.

Adam once more took up their tour of the village. He was more formal now. How quickly he had learned the expectations of a person of rank. He maintained his personable and deeper connections with her and Lord and Lady Jonquil. But what if he continued to keep everyone else at a distance? He would be very lonely indeed.

Mr. Simpkin leaned a touch closer to her as they walked and whispered, "You look pensive. Is something the matter?"

"I worry about the wee boy," she said. "Always."

"You needn't worry right this moment. He is happy and looked after and is having an adventure and a pleasant excursion. Let your mind rest a bit."

She appreciated the sentiment behind his words. There would be time enough for worrying. For now, she could breathe.

"What else did Lord Jonquil show you when you were here?" she asked Adam.

He led them about, indicating shops and things of interest. He didn't fully warm up to Mr. Simpkin, but he did relax a bit. All in all, they spent a very lovely time in the village.

They met the coachman at the previously decided upon place. He'd spent his time in the pub but wasn't in his cups.

The pony cart was not large enough for Mr. Simpkin, Adam, and Robbie to all ride in the back without Adam sitting on her lap. She suspected he didn't appreciate the babyish arrangement, but he acquiesced. The road back was bumpy and at times unforgiving. She wrapped one arm around Adam, worrying he'd be bumped clear out.

At first, he was stiff and didn't seem to appreciate her protective gesture. But after a moment he set his arms around hers and leaned back against her as he used to do. His eyes were on the mountain, the one he had climbed with Lord Jonquil. She suspected his thoughts were even further afield. The times she caught him with this particular pensive expression, she knew he was thinking of his father. She held him tighter, wishing she could take away his heartache.

In a low voice, she sang to him the song she had since he was born, one that never failed to calm him.

Saw ye my wee thing? Saw ye my own thing?
Saw ye my bonnie boy down by the lea?
He skipped 'cross the meadow yestere'en at the gloaming.
Small as a thistle my dear boy is he.

Adam sniffled a little, curling himself against her. She pressed a little kiss to the top of his head. That he didn't object, he who wouldn't even let her hold his hand lately, spoke volumes of his heavy heart.

Mr. Simpkin set his hand around her free one. He didn't say anything but simply offered support. She had come to realize he was very observant and hardly missed a thing. He had seemed to sort out that she was grieving. Though she was generally a very private person and kept to herself, she accepted the comfort he offered and laid her head against his shoulder.

They rode like that all the way back to Brier Hill. Leaning into the strength of this good-hearted man, with a child resting on her lap, Robbie could almost picture herself with the family she'd never have. Servants didn't marry. And they didn't have children. If she took up employment as a nursemaid again, this little dream she'd never let fully blossom in her heart could never become reality. But she had no other skills. And leaving Adam would devastate him.

If only life were as easy to sort as a surprise Christmas celebration.

Chapter Ten

Miss MacGregor had Howard thinking any number of foolish things. He'd never before sat beside a woman as she sang to comfort a child. That moment had etched itself into his mind and, stranger still, into his heart. He'd never before let himself imagine being part of a moment like that, and now he could think of little else.

Rain had begun falling not long after they'd returned to Brier Hill. Howard wasn't averse to working in the rain—he'd never accomplish anything otherwise—but this was a downpour of near-biblical proportions. He'd resigned himself to spending the remainder of the day in his coach-turned-house. His attempt at distracting himself with a bit of whittling was proving futile. That, of course, was likely owing to the fact that what he was carving was a toy horse for the young duke.

> *Saw ye my wee thing? Saw ye my own thing?*
> *Saw ye my bonnie boy down by the lea?*
> *He skipped 'cross the meadow yestere'en at the gloaming.*
> *Small as a thistle my dear boy is he.*

He smiled to himself as Miss MacGregor's voice echoed in his mind. What else did she sing? Was she one to hum while she worked? He'd enjoyed talking with her as they'd worked in the garden, and he was intrigued at the idea of music filling a moment like that.

Quit your foolishness, now.

He had nothing but this oddity of a house and a life of constant change to offer a woman. He wasn't poor, but he was far from wealthy. Though he'd not yet reached forty, he knew that years spent laboring in the sun, hefting heavy loads, and working himself to the bone had aged him. Any woman would hesitate when faced with those things.

And this woman had more reasons than those. To build a life with someone, she'd have to stop working as a nursemaid. She couldn't keep living at or near Falstone Castle. Building a life elsewhere meant leaving her beloved little duke. She would never do that.

It likely didn't matter either way. He'd no assurance she felt the same pull toward him that he had begun to feel for her. And there he was, already pondering futures. Foolishness upon foolishness.

Howard pushed thoughts of singing and smiles and fiery Scotswomen from his mind and focused fully on his whittling. He managed it for a full five minutes when a knock sounded on the door of his carriage house.

Who could possibly be venturing out in weather like this?

He opened the door slowly because it opened outward and most people weren't expecting that.

"Miss MacGregor." The shock of seeing her there froze him. He quickly recollected himself, though, and pulled her inside and out of the rain. "You might've drowned trying to get here."

"I am a right good swimmer."

He latched the door against the gusts of wet wind. "Are you, now?"

"Actually, no."

"Something important must have convinced you to brave the elements."

She nodded. "Lady Jonquil said she is fond of . . ." Her brow tugged in thought. "I was so careful to repeat it over and over so I'd nae forget." She bounced in place, rubbing at her arms.

"Heavens, you're soaked." He'd been too thrown off his guard to notice sooner.

Howard tucked back the curtain dividing the sitting area of his odd little house from his sleeping quarters and grabbed his blanket. The curtain fell back into place as he turned toward his shivering visitor.

He wrapped the blanket around her.

"Thank you." She spoke with such exhausted gratitude that he felt ever more guilty for not having realized her misery sooner. "While we were working on decorations for Adam's Christmas party, Lady Jonquil said she's fond of a flower called queen of the meadow, and her brother sent seeds back to England when he was away in the colonies. You're planting a flower for Lord Jonquil. I thought you could plant this one for her, if Lord Jonquil will allow you to have some of the seeds."

She had run through the rain to help him with his garden? What a remarkable thing to do.

She continued. "I don't know what that flower looks like or if the seeds'll still grow anything after so many years, but I thought you'd want to know."

He opened the drawer where he kept his drawing supplies. "I should bring you with me on all my jobs; you could be my spy."

"I'd do a fine job of it."

"Queen of the meadow looks like this." He quickly sketched the flower, one few people were familiar with. "The flowers start as tight balls and grow as dozens of tiny blooms on a stalk. When they open, each petal is a near-perfect circle. Long stamens emerge from the center, always in a different color from the petals."

She studied his sketch as he worked at it. "What color is the flower?"

"They come in a variety: white, pink, purple."

"The stamen looks almost like a crown." She smiled at him. "Perhaps that's the reason for its name."

"Might very well be."

Her fingers peeked out from beneath the blanket, holding it in place around her. "Where in the garden ought they to be planted?"

"They need soil that remains quite moist, so they'd do best in the shade." He pulled out the garden plan and unrolled it on his small table. "This flower bed, here, would be a good choice."

She came closer once more, standing very near him to look at his plans. "Why not plant them in the same bed as the forget-me-nots? Those are Lady Jonquil's favorite. Planting the two together would make that corner of the garden hers, in a way. I think she and her husband would both like the thought of that."

"Brilliant."

A droplet of water fell on the table by his plans, narrowly missing the paper. He stood and turned toward her, fully meaning to tease her about bringing the weather in with her, but she was closer than he'd realized. Her cheeks were rosy from the cold, and the rain had brought out the curl in her hair. Her deep brown eyes were fixed on him, the flicker of lantern light reflected in their depths.

"I wish my little stove put out more heat," he said. "You're soaked quite through."

Her smile was soft. "The blanket helps."

She was shivering though. He set his hands on her arms hidden beneath the blanket and rubbed them.

"Is Robbie your given name?" he asked.

She shook her head. "Roberta."

"Roberta," he repeated, liking the sound of it. "That name suits you."

"It didn't when I was a wee lassie."

He could appreciate that. "When I was small, I was called Howie. That name would never do now."

"Howard?" She seemed quite sure of her guess.

"What else?"

His hands slowed as his mind began spinning on the reality of her there, visiting with him, standing close, smiling at him.

"Thank you for holding my hand today in the pony cart," she said. "I was fretting myself into a terrible worry."

"I suspected as much."

She raised herself on her toes and brushed a kiss to his cheek. The rat-a-tat rhythm of his heart picked up pace. He stood as still as a tree on a breezeless day, not by choice but out of sheer shock. He'd not expected such a tender gesture. Even less expected was how much he enjoyed it.

Robbie spun his blanket off her shoulders and slipped quickly from the carriage house and out into the rain, leaving him behind with his whirling thoughts.

Those lofty thoughts he'd had before her arrival hadn't disappeared in the least. Rather, they'd grown into cloud-built castles, and he hadn't the first idea what to do about it.

Chapter Eleven

Everyone at Brier Hill was being very strange. Adam usually spent his afternoons with someone, but Nurse Robbie had insisted he stay in his guest bedchamber and read a book. He didn't mind reading; he'd always liked it. He found he liked it even more knowing that Lady Jonquil was also fond of reading.

But he didn't want to be reading just now. He wanted to be with the others, which was a new thing for him. Adam was like his father in that way: he enjoyed quiet. Father had often said as much, and he was never ashamed that the two of them liked to keep to themselves.

"I require people," Mother had once said to his father.

But dukes didn't need people. Father had taught him that.

Why, then, did he want so badly to be with the rest of the Brier Hill household?

He climbed off his chair and walked over to the window. This window didn't look out on the mountain he'd walked on with Lord Jonquil, but it did offer a view of the front of the estate. It was pretty. A little breeze was making the branches on the trees sway, and there were lots of flowers. Adam liked Brier Hill. He hoped Nurse Robbie was right, that Lord and Lady Jonquil would invite them to come back again. He and Nurse Robbie would be very happy to visit over and over.

The door to the room opened. He turned and looked, unsure who it would be.

Nurse Robbie stood in the doorway. She smiled at him. She'd been happier since they'd come to Brier Hill. Nurse Robbie should always come with him when he visited here. Then they would be happy together. It was the perfect arrangement.

"Come with me, wee Adam. We've something wonderful waiting for you."

"What is it?" he asked.

She shook her head, smiling all the broader. "I'll nae tell you. You have to come and discover for yourself."

He stood firm. "I don't like to be surprised."

Nurse Robbie held her hand out to him. "I know you don't, but sometimes life is surprising. This will be good practice."

He supposed she was right about that. Life did surprise him sometimes, usually unpleasantly.

With the firmly set shoulders and very serious mouth he'd seen his father use, Adam walked through the door. Nurse Robbie dropped her hand away. He felt bad about that. She was always trying to hold his hand. But he wasn't a little boy anymore. He was a duke. Dukes didn't hold people's hands.

They walked together to the stairs and down to the ground floor. Nurse Robbie motioned for him to go into the sitting room where they always gathered after supper each night. He stepped inside.

The room was decorated . . . for Christmas. Pine boughs rested on the mantelpiece above the fireplace. An evergreen wreath hung on a wall. Arrangements of other branches and flowers in the colors and jolliness of the holy season filled the room. There were even presents.

"I don't understand," he said.

"You missed Christmas," Lady Jonquil said. "You ought not to miss Christmas."

Adam looked up at Nurse Robbie, hoping she would explain further.

"When Lord and Lady Jonquil heard you'd not been at home for the Christmas festivities, they determined we'd have a Christmas celebration here, now."

He looked back at his host and hostess. They looked eager and enthusiastic. Nurse Robbie seemed excited at the idea of Christmas in April. Mr. Simpkin was there as well, which would not have been Adam's preference. But his heart was starting to swell up with the idea of Christmas, and he was too pleased to even mind Mr. Simpkin being there.

"Is it to be a true Christmastime celebration, with stories and wassail and such?" He held his breath for the answer.

"Of course," Lord Jonquil said quickly and eagerly. "We can play any and all games we wish. We can sing songs and tell stories. Cook has made wassail since Nurse Robbie told us that is a favorite at Falstone Castle. We also have ginger biscuits because those are a favorite of Lady Jonquil's."

Adam turned to her. "I didn't know that."

She smiled and nodded. "I have enjoyed them since I was a little girl."

"What is your decision, my wee Adam?" Nurse Robbie asked. "Are we to have a special Christmas celebration?"

He wanted to simply jump into the festivities, to eagerly embrace the possibility of something so joyful. But what if he were disappointed? What if they got partway through and everyone else decided they didn't want to keep going? He didn't want to get his hopes up only to have them dashed to pieces.

"It is probably ridiculous to have Christmas in April," he said.

Lady Jonquil gave him one of her soft smiles. "There is nothing ridiculous about Christmas. And celebrating it is a wonderful thing, no matter when that celebration occurs."

"We should begin with the presents," Lord Jonquil suggested, wiggling his eyebrows. "Don't you think so, Adam?"

Presents. Oh dear. "I didn't get presents for anyone."

Lady Jonquil motioned him to the fireplace and the table near it with wrapped parcels atop. "The presents were never meant to be *from* you, but *for* you."

"They're all for me?" He'd never have imagined such a thing.

Lord Jonquil sat on the floor, much as he had when they'd played with tops after Adam first arrived. He tapped the floor near him. "Have a seat."

"On the floor?" He'd never sat on the floor during Christmas at the castle.

"Where else would a highwayman sit?" Lord Jonquil didn't hide his grin.

Adam felt a smile pull at his own lips. "Are we being highwaymen tonight?"

Lord Jonquil shrugged. "Maybe a little. We'd best retain some dignity, on account of the both of us being very fine and titled gentlemen."

"We can be highwaymen when we're walking on the mountain," Adam suggested.

"Excellent idea."

Adam sat on the floor, watching the people around him, both confused and excited.

Lady Jonquil handed him a present shaped precisely like a book. He removed the paper around it to discover it was, in fact, a book. But not just any book. It was *The History of Little Goody Two-Shoes*, the book he'd been reading with her.

"We'll continue reading it while you're here, of course," she said. "But you are enjoying it so much that I want you to have it forever and ever."

He wanted to ask if he could bring it back with him when he visited. He wanted to ask so he would know if they meant to allow him to return. But he didn't dare. He didn't want to be sad on a night when they were going to celebrate Christmas.

Lord Jonquil gave him another wrapped present. It was soft. The outside wasn't paper but black fabric. Presents weren't usually wrapped in black.

Adam untied the ribbon around it, and the wrapping unrolled into a long, narrow strip of fabric.

"You needed a highwayman sash to tie about your waist," Lord Jonquil said in that tone he used when he was being funny but pretending to be very serious.

"And it has to be black so people know I'm still sad about my father." Adam would have to keep wearing black for months and months. It was the rules. His heart was very sad, so he didn't mind wearing sad colors. It would have been ridiculous not to.

"After you are no longer required to wear black," Lord Jonquil said, "you can still use it as your pirate sash because it will be very intimidating."

Adam liked that. "I would be a very frightening highwayman."

"And every highwayman would be afraid of crossing you." Lord Jonquil looked like he thought that a fine thing.

"I could drive about with my ducal arms on the carriage and flags flying, and all the highwaymen would hide instead of robbing me." That was the way a duke ought to ride about the kingdom. "And then, because they were afraid of me, I could sneak people away from them so those people wouldn't get hurt. And the highwaymen would have to stop hurting people."

Lady Jonquil sat on the floor beside him, the sides of her blue silk dress bubbling up beside her. She pulled him into a hug. "Oh, my brave Adam. You have the best and bravest heart of any boy I've ever known."

He didn't always like to be hugged, but he liked it then. He leaned up against her and smiled.

"This here's from me." Mr. Simpkin handed him a present.

Adam untied the twine bow. He peeled back the bit of paper wrapped around the oddly shaped item. Inside was a horse carved from a very dark wood. Its legs were in a running position. He'd never had a wooden horse that didn't look like it was standing about being bored. This horse looked exciting and strong.

"Thank you," he said.

"My pleasure, Your Grace." Mr. Simpkin had to call him that, but he made it sound more like a name than a title, like it was something he said because he was a friend.

"And, my wee Adam, this is from me." Nurse Robbie gave him a handkerchief, one that was very white, so it must have been very new.

Adam unfolded it. One corner was embroidered with a letter *K*, with loops and extra bits to make it fancy.

"The *K* is for Kielder," she explained.

That made a lot of sense. The opposite corner of the handkerchief had an embroidered thistle.

"The thistle because of your song?" he asked. "The one you sing to me?"

Nurse Robbie nodded. "I sewed it for you these last few nights after you'd gone to sleep."

"My father always had a handkerchief."

Lord Jonquil nodded with approval. "Gentlemen always carry them."

"That's one of the rules?" Adam asked.

"It is. And Nurse Robbie has made certain you have one that suits you."

Adam looked to his beloved nurse once more. "Thank you, Nurse Robbie."

"Of course, my wee boy."

Lord Jonquil stood, something he always did with a bounce. He never did seem able to sit still for very long. "We should play a game."

"I like games," Adam said, still leaning against Lady Jonquil with her arms holding him soft and gentle.

"I know which one," she said. "Masked tag."

"I'm devilishly fond of masked tag." Lord Jonquil spoke excitedly. Whatever game this new one was, it must be quite enjoyable. "What do you say, Adam? Would you like to play masked tag?"

"I don't know what that is," he admitted without embarrassment. He was too excited to be embarrassed.

"You might know it by another name," Lady Jonquil said. "I've heard it called many different things. One of the people playing has a piece of cloth tied over his or her eyes so he or she cannot see. The others stand nearby, calling out to the one who is searching for them but all the while attempting to avoid being caught. If someone is caught and the one doing the catching can identify that person, they switch places."

Adam thought he understood, but he was a little confused. "Is this a fun game?"

Lord and Lady Jonquil looked confused.

"Have you never played it?" she asked.

Adam shook his head. "My father didn't play very many games with me. I'm not sure he understood about games. There weren't any other children at the castle. My mother wasn't—"

His voice broke off the way it sometimes did when he talked about her. He didn't know if she would have played with him if she'd ever been at home. He wasn't certain she liked spending time with him.

Of all people, Mr. Simpkin saved Adam from his sudden dip into embarrassment.

"I'll be the first to do the seeking," he stood. "I was quite good at this game when I was a young boy."

Arrangements were made quickly for Mr. Simpkin's eyes to be covered with the black sash Adam had been given. While that was being accomplished, Adam had a chance to regain his footing. He didn't always grow emotional when talking about his mother, but he had just done so. Perhaps it was because he was finally having the Christmas he'd missed. He remembered the loneliness of being in that cold boardinghouse with no other boys around, eating alone—even the matron who ran it hadn't joined him—listening to the silence all around him and wishing he'd been having Christmas with his mother.

Here, though, he wasn't alone. Decorations filled the room. He'd had presents. They were going to play a game. Lady Jonquil had said Christmas wasn't ridiculous. Adam had his suspicions Christmas was actually rather magical.

Masked tag was not a difficult game, he discovered. One simply had to move quickly. He was good at that part. Mr. Simpkin caught and identified Lady Jonquil, who then caught and identified her husband. All the while, Adam kept enough away not to be caught himself. He even grew a bit bolder in calling out to the one doing the seeking.

Lord Jonquil spun about very suddenly and snatched hold of him.

"This can't be Mr. Simpkin," he said. "Mr. Simpkin is much smaller."

Adam then did something he could remember doing only a few times in all his life: he laughed. He laughed from deep in his belly. The laughter rushed out of him before he could stop it. Then, without warning, the laughing turned to crying.

As embarrassed as he had been while talking about his mother, these tears were humiliating. Without a word, Lord Jonquil tugged the black cloth away from his eyes, snatched Adam into his arms, and pulled him into a fierce and protective hug.

Adam wrapped his arms around his neck and held on as if his life depended upon not letting go. He hadn't the courage to look at the others. If they were eyeing him with pity or, worse yet, mocking his sorrow, he'd be devastated. So he buried his face against Lord Jonquil and pretended no one else was nearby.

"Perhaps it is time for telling stories," Lady Jonquil suggested.

Lord Jonquil sat on a nearby chair, still holding Adam. Father had sometimes held him like this. It was a different hug from Lady Jonquil's. Hers felt like a soft, warm blanket. Lord Jonquil's felt like being safe.

"You can use your handkerchief to wipe at your eyes," Lord Jonquil said. "That's one reason we carry them."

"I'm sorry," Adam whispered.

"For what, sweeting?"

"For crying on you."

Lord Jonquil held him ever tighter. "The most important thing a person can do when he feels the need to cry is to cry."

"Even dukes?" he asked, his voice tinier than he liked it to be.

"Maybe *especially* dukes." Lord Jonquil also spoke soft and small.

Adam curled into him, clutching the handkerchief. He wasn't to be scolded or sent away. And Lord Jonquil wasn't talking about this so loudly that others would overhear. Adam had spent so much of the months since his father's death fighting for himself. Feeling protected was a welcome change.

"I'll tell the first story," Lady Jonquil said. "I know a wonderfully funny one about Lord Jonquil."

Adam could feel the gentleman in question laugh, though he did so silently. He'd never experienced that before. It made him smile even with tears still wetting his cheeks.

"When Lord Jonquil was about fourteen years old," Lady Jonquil said, "he and my brother, Stanley, decided that they were going to set up a house of their own in the boathouse at Lampton Park, where Lord Jonquil then lived."

Adam turned the tiniest bit, just enough to hear her better. Lord Jonquil kept his arms around him, but not forcefully.

"They gathered blankets and changes of clothing. Determined to feed themselves as well, they made certain the boathouse contained fishing poles and nets. They slipped a backgammon board from Farland Meadows into the boathouse for entertainment. They were even thorough enough to make certain they had a lantern for light."

Adam looked at Lord Jonquil. "You were like highwaymen with a hideaway."

He nodded. "Stanley knew how to have the best adventures."

"What the two of them didn't think of, though," Lady Jonquil continued, "was what would happen if their plans were discovered by . . . Lord Jonquil's younger brother."

Adam turned his eyes on the gentleman again. "You had a younger brother?"

"Two, in fact. And a little sister."

It was probably a good thing Adam didn't have any brothers or sisters. They would be alone now too. And they would be sad. And Nurse Robbie would be overwhelmed looking after all of them.

"His brother James discovered their plans and hatched one of his own." Lady Jonquil's voice had grown mysterious.

Adam turned and faced her.

"He decided he was going to scare them. So, late on the night they settled in at the boathouse, he hid beneath the only window in the building and waited for their lantern to be extinguished."

Again, Adam could feel Lord Jonquil silently laughing. And again it made him smile.

"James had brought a lantern." Lady Jonquil looked at Adam as she told her story. "Holding it near enough to oddly light his face, he slowly stood, framing his face in the window, the only thing visible there to the two boys inside."

Adam looked up at Lord Jonquil. "What did you do?"

"We screamed." He laughed out loud at that. "He played quite the trick on us. Scared us near out of our wits. Once we realized he was the specter in the window, we dashed from the boathouse and chased him all over the grounds. It was quite a lark."

In the very next instant, the housekeeper arrived with a tray, one side of it holding a plate of ginger biscuits and the other two rows of glasses. Following right behind her was the butler, carrying a bowl of wassail.

"Do you feel ready to have some biscuits and wassail?" Lord Jonquil asked him quietly.

"Yes, please."

The arms that had kept him warm and reassured dropped away. He climbed down and crossed to the table to claim his Christmas goodies.

Everyone was talking and smiling. Lady Jonquil expressed her delight at having her favorite ginger biscuits. Adam took small sips of the hot apple drink, the taste reminding him of his Christmases with Father at Falstone Castle. It made him a little sad, but it also felt nice to enjoy part of it again in a place that was so happy.

He set his glass down and walked over to Lady Jonquil. He tugged lightly on her dress when she didn't realize he was there. She turned toward him, and her eyes brightened when she saw him. She always looked excited when she saw him. He liked that.

"Thank you for Christmas," he said.

Lord Jonquil stepped over to them and set his arm around his wife. "This has been a beautiful Christmas celebration." To Adam, specifically, he said, "Thank you for sharing it with us."

Adam wasn't one who smiled often, but he couldn't help himself just then. Every bit of him felt happy. Everything about that moment felt perfect.

"I suspect," Lord Jonquil said with a little laugh, "Mr. Simpkin and Nurse Robbie wish we'd managed to find some mistletoe."

"Why is that?" Adam wasn't certain what Lord Jonquil was trying to say.

"It is a tradition at Christmastime," Lord Jonquil said, "for a couple who are caught under a sprig of mistletoe to exchange a kiss."

Adam looked over at Nurse Robbie and Mr. Simpkin, who were standing beside one another, talking with the butler and housekeeper. "Why would they want to kiss each other?"

"I believe," Lady Jonquil said, "they are falling in love."

Falling in love? Adam hadn't thought that. He hoped it wasn't true. When people fell in love, they often married. And when people got married, they went away.

But Nurse Robbie wouldn't leave him; he knew she wouldn't. She loved him. He was her wee Adam. And she was the only person who had never left him behind.

Chapter Twelve

The Christmas celebration had gone as well as Robbie had hoped. Better, in many ways. Adam had clearly been confused at first, but he'd quickly embraced the joy of it. Watching him play with such abandon and glee had done her heart good. He'd always been such a serious child. With so few opportunities to play with other children, he didn't really know how.

Lord Jonquil was proving an oddly perfect playmate. He'd a restless joyfulness about him that was infectious. His boundless enthusiasm helped Adam feel courage enough to participate in something so unfamiliar to him. But the gentleman was also attentive and quick to address the wee boy's struggles and concerns.

Again and again her thoughts had returned to that moment when, without warning, Adam had burst into tears. Lord Jonquil had held him and comforted him precisely the way a loving father would. Seeing it had offered Robbie's heart a little respite from the worry that had rested there for months. She felt so terribly alone in her efforts to give Adam stability and reassurance.

She stood at a small window near the back of the house. Though she told herself she hadn't any particular reason for placing herself in that specific spot, the more honest part of her knew why she was there. Through the glass she could catch the smallest glimpse of Howard working out in the garden corner. His stone had finally arrived, and he'd hired on local men to help with building the garden wall. They were making quick headway. She enjoyed watching him take pleasure and satisfaction in his work.

Adam had spent time that morning studying the horse Howard had carved for him. He'd listed for Robbie all the bits of it he found interesting or lifelike. Her little lad appreciated the gift, and receiving it served as a testimonial that he was thought of and cared about. What a good and kind man Howard was proving himself to be.

And, oh, the tender moment they'd shared the night it had rained. Warmth spread from the top of her head to the tips of her toes every time she thought back on it. Nothing in that brief touch of his arms to hers and her lips to his cheek ought to've impacted her as much as it had, and yet she felt in many ways as if everything had changed in the length of those few breaths.

Into her reverie came the sound of footsteps. She assumed a neutral expression and looked over her shoulder to see who was passing by. It was Lady Jonquil. She didn't continue on her way but stopped at the window as well.

"Forgive the intrusion," she said.

Flustered and a bit embarrassed, Robbie said, "Nothing to interrupt, I assure you."

The lady nodded but not as if she fully believed Robbie's assertion. "I've been meaning to ask you, since you are better acquainted with Her Grace than I am, whether or not you think she is likely to allow Adam to spend his school holidays here. We would very much like him to do so whenever possible. Obviously, sometimes it won't be feasible. But when he can stay with us, we would like for him to."

That did Robbie's heart good, but her mind immediately pointed out a coming difficulty. "You will soon enough have a bairn of your own to look after. As your family grows, having Adam among your number will grow less convenient."

Lady Jonquil did not look discouraged. Indeed, she appeared almost amused. "My husband and I both came from large families, at least compared to others of our station, and we hope to have a large family of our own. A bit of chaos will hardly sink us."

"Adam is not likely to invite chaos. He's far more likely to be overlooked."

Lady Jonquil shook her head. "He is quiet, yes, but even at only eight years old he has a presence. He may be overlooked now, but were I one to place wagers, I'd bet every shilling to my name that he will grow up to be a gentleman no one overlooks."

"I suppose it is difficult for me to imagine him grown. I still sometimes think of him as the tiny infant I used to hold."

"I suppose that contradiction is difficult to reconcile for many people. In time, children become adults." And then, her voice a little quieter, she added, "If life is kind."

She seemed to shake off the heaviness of that observation. Her face lightened once more. This was a lady who'd known sorrow and had found a way to continue on. It was little wonder she'd so easily recognized the grief Adam felt.

"Would you accompany me a moment?" she asked. "There is something else I wish to ask you."

Robbie agreed. The two of them walked away from the window and to the staircase, with its intricate carved flowers.

"Before I ask my question," Lady Jonquil said, "I must make a somewhat indelicate observation."

What could that possibly be?

"Upon your arrival here, I realized you are younger than I thought when I first saw you for that brief moment at Falstone Castle. In my defense, the room you were in was poorly lit, the morning was quite early, and without divulging too many personal secrets, I was struggling with a very heavy worry at the time. My mind was not entirely clear."

"I am not offended," Robbie reassured her. With a smile, she added, "The fact that you offered up poor lighting as an excuse for my apparently elderly appearance does wonders for my potentially battered confidence."

"I thank you for your generosity. My reason for making the observation is that I had thought you might not be interested in a new position after your time ends at Falstone Castle, which, considering Adam is at the age when he would have a governess, is likely soon. But you are quite young enough to be anticipating many more years as a nursemaid."

They crossed through a small antechamber, with two doors on either side. Lady Jonquil led the way to the door on the right. The bedchamber beyond, with its soft fabrics and dressing table with lady's toilette accessories, must have been Lady Jonquil's. They passed through it and through yet another door. This one led to a cozily appointed sitting room, perfectly circular in shape, with one section of the walls made entirely of windows. The view was breathtaking: the mountains in the distance, the grounds of the estate spread out below.

"We will be welcoming our addition to our family before the year is out." Lady Jonquil brushed her hand lightly over her middle, something she likely didn't realize she did somewhat regularly. "If you are interested in continuing to work as a nursemaid, we would be deeply grateful if you would consider the possibility of coming here. As I said, we hope ours will be a large family. You would have a secure position for years to come if that's what you want."

Though servants didn't usually speak about personal matters with people of Lady Jonquil's station, Robbie couldn't help being as forthcoming as the lady had been with her. "I'll confess, my lady, you've hit upon a matter I've been pondering myself. My time with Adam will be over soon enough—there's no avoiding that—but I'm nae certain what I hope lies ahead for me. I'm far more worried about what lies ahead for him." Robbie realized something. "If I am here as a nursemaid, he would see me regularly too."

"Please do not think that is the only reason we have extended the offer. I have seen again and again your kind tenderness and your willingness to help Adam do difficult things, and he clearly loves you and depends on you. That speaks highly of you as a nursemaid. That the arrangement would allow Adam to continue to have you in his life is simply an additional benefit."

Robbie paced a little bit away. "I have enjoyed being a nursemaid, but . . ." How could she explain her hesitancy to accept a position that anyone else in her situation would've dropped to their knees in gratitude to have been offered?

"But your thoughts have begun turning to even more pleasant possibilities?" Lady Jonquil said.

Robbie felt a bit at a loss for words. Admitting to the feelings she herself had only just begun to recognize froze her tongue.

"Lest you think I am shocked or horrified or disapproving"—the lady motioned to the wall of windows—"I brought you here because I felt it would be more conducive to your efforts than your previous location."

Robbie crossed to the windows and looked out. She needed but a moment to understand Lady Jonquil's purpose. These windows offered a full view of the workers on the grounds. She could see all they were doing, all that was being accomplished. She could see Howard as he walked about offering instructions and assistance. This was not the tiny glimpse through an awkwardly placed window she had afforded herself below.

"I hadn't come here expecting this."

"Do you mean you hadn't come to this room expecting this view?" Lady Jonquil asked. "Or that you hadn't come to Brier Hill expecting to meet someone like Mr. Simpkin?" There was no mocking in the question, only heartfelt compassion.

"Both," Robbie admitted. "I don't know how to proceed. I do think he has many of the same feelings for me that I do for him. There is a possibility that, if those feelings grow, we could build a life together. I very much like the idea of that."

Lady Jonquil did not offer her own thoughts or make any effort to interrupt. She simply listened.

"Adam has a degree of dislike for him, though I'm at a loss as to why." She shook her head. "I don't think there is anything about Howard—Mr. Simpkin's character that warrants that distrust. I cannot sort out why Adam dislikes him."

"You have been with Adam every day of his life until he was sent away to school. I suspect he jealously guards his time with you now that you are together again. He is a very perceptive boy, more even than most. He may have sensed even before you did the tug you felt toward 'Howard.'"

"And if something does grow between Howard and me, I'd very seldom see Adam." She sighed. "No matter what I choose, someone'll be unhappy."

"And has the necessity of making this choice been presented to you already?" Again, Lady Jonquil managed to pose a question very delicately that could have, if not made with care, sounded like a criticism.

"No. Howard's nae made any offers or proposals."

"Perhaps a solution will present itself before that bridge is unavoidably before you." Lady Jonquil motioned subtly to the window. "Please remain here as long as you wish. I often stand here and watch my husband as he plays with the dog. There is something peaceful and joyous in simply seeing the person you love."

Robbie nodded. She understood that well.

"And while you enjoy the afternoon's respite," Lady Jonquil added, "I intend to write a letter."

"To whom?" Robbie asked.

"To a certain duchess to whom I mean to insist that a certain little duke be permitted to come here from Harrow whenever possible."

"*Insist* rather than *ask*?"

"Mine is often a quiet disposition," Lady Jonquil said. "But I am more than capable of being fierce when I need to be. And that little boy needs me to be."

With that, Lady Jonquil slipped from the room, her posture one of a warrior.

Robbie turned her attention to the garden below and took comfort in seeing Howard there, so confident and sure and steady.

If the duchess would allow Adam to spend at least some holidays with Lord and Lady Jonquil, then Robbie no longer being at the castle would not be so devastating a blow to the wee boy. If she were *here*, Adam would have her every bit as much in his life as he would if she remained at Falstone.

She did not yet know what the future might hold, but two distinct possibilities lay ahead of her: a life with Howard, if he offered, traveling the kingdom and building gardens together. Or a nursemaid here at Brier Hill as part of the Jonquil family and part of Adam's life.

There was happiness and sorrow to be had down both paths, and she hadn't yet the first idea which would prove hers in the end.

Chapter Thirteen

Howard had received his share of attention from the girls his age when he'd been a young man. He'd puffed up a bit when he'd caught any of them watching him. Experiencing it again now was proving quite enjoyable. Robbie had stood at the tall windows at the back of the house, one story above the ground, for quite a while that afternoon. Though he suspected she might have set her gaze on other things as well, he had every confidence she'd been watching him. Watching him *with pleasure*, he hoped.

The evening was waning on, and he alone was in the garden, finishing his work for the day. Robbie had abandoned her post, but he had not forgotten the joy of seeing her there. The smile simply refused to leave his face. He suspected she wasn't the sort who grew quickly or frequently lovestruck. The same could be said of him. And yet how quickly his heart had grown fond of her, something he felt certain was mutual. The idea kept him inwardly grinning as he saw to his tasks.

Amid his smiles and tasks, the object of his pleasant thoughts arrived in the garden, with a basket hanging over one arm. "You never stopped for tea," she said.

She *had* been watching him. Howard let the corner of his mouth tug upward.

"I suspect you've not paused for your evening meal either." Robbie made her way closer to where he stood, basket swaying in time with the edges of her dress.

"I've not had a moment yet to return to my carriage home and fill my belly."

Robbie clicked her tongue and shook her head. "I hope I'm not to discover you're one for neglecting your health in favor of your work."

"I'm not, generally." He dropped his voice the tiniest bit. "But I've had a rather fine distraction today."

Two splotches of color answered that bit of flirting. "I've found myself a wee bit distracted today as well."

"Have you?"

Those bewitching eyes of hers danced even as she clearly fought a smile of her own. "I filched a few things from the kitchen and brought them out with me." She held the basket up. "You've time for a bite to eat, I hope."

"That'd depend a great deal on whether I'd be eating alone." Lands, it'd been a time since he'd flirted so shamelessly. Truth be told, he was enjoying it.

"I could send the dog over," Robbie said, tossing him a bit of a saucy look. "Pooka's fond of a meal, I'd wager."

"Not at all what I had in mind." Howard chuckled and did his best to clean the dirt from his hands with his far-from-elegant handkerchief. "Have you time enough for a bite to eat?"

She smiled at last. "I'd planned to eat with you, assuming you wanted me to."

His hands as clean as they were likely to get, he tucked the bit of well-worn cloth into his waistcoat pocket. "I'd fancy having a meal with you, Robbie MacGregor."

"Then I'd suggest you find me a place to sit that's not muddy."

"I know just the spot." He held his hand out to her.

She set her hand in his without hesitation or uncertainty. That hadn't happened in ages, not since he was a very young man with so little to offer that even holding hands with him was seen as a comedown for any young woman.

He led them from the garden he was building to a nearby corner of the lawn where a wooden bench waited to be sat upon.

Robbie placed the basket on her lap and pulled back the cloth tucked into the top of it. "Cook had a couple of meat pies she let me sneak off with."

"Is our little duke taking his meal with Lord and Lady Jonquil?" Howard knew little ones generally ate in their nursery with their nursemaids. He couldn't imagine the unconventional lord and lady of this house allowing such a thing.

"He is," Robbie said. "And quite pleased with himself over it."

"And *I'm* quite pleased to be taking my meal with *you*."

Robbie looked up from her basket. "When I first met you, Howard Simpkin, I'd not have believed you had a knack for velvety words."

"I can't say I'd been prone to them before meeting you."

"And I hadn't near so much love for gardens," she said, handing him one of the meat pies.

"It's the gardens you're fond of?"

An obvious war being fought between her instinct to smile and her apparent determination not to, Robbie asked, "What else could I possibly be fond enough of to drag a basket of meat pies from the house?"

"Give me a chance this evening," he said, "and I'll see if I can't sort out the answer to that question."

"I think I'd like that." She took out her meat pie, then set the basket on the ground beside them.

"What else do you like, Robbie?" Howard truly wanted to know. He liked everything he'd learned of her and felt certain he would like everything he'd yet discover.

"The smell of rain," she said. "Thick-sliced bread. Clotted cream."

He nodded slowly, remembering all those things with pleasure of his own. "I haven't had clotted cream in ages. But the smell of rain . . ." He sighed. "I know that well."

"I'd wager at times you're not terribly pleased that rain's falling."

He laughed lightly. "Ill-timed rain isn't a favorite of mine, I'll admit. But rain that comes after a garden's completed is, in my estimation, the best sort of sign. The rain will make the garden bloom."

"Does it ever make you sad that you aren't there to see those gardens bloom? You do so much work, but you don't get to see it."

"Planting isn't about what's happening in the moment; it's believing in the future."

They'd both been eating their pies as they talked. Her expression turned thoughtful, but she'd only just taken a bite and didn't say what was on her mind.

"Does your little duke enjoy gardens?" he asked. "It might do him good to find something hopeful in the future with so much sorrow in his past."

She swallowed. "I can't say he's spent much time in gardens. My wee boy gets overwhelmed quickly by unfamiliar things."

"So long as I'm one of those 'unfamiliar things,' I suspect he'll not overly take to me." He could not possibly have mistaken the wariness His Grace felt, but the boy had seemed to like his little carved horse. That might help a bit. "We made some progress during our Christmas celebration."

"It seems to me Christmas is magical no matter when we celebrate it," Robbie said.

"Did you enjoy our Christmas festivities?" Howard asked.

She smiled at him. "I did indeed. Greenery and stories and wassail."

"And the company of a delightful gardener, of course." He winked at her.

Robbie smiled as wide as the River Tyne. "I've not been winked at since I was sixteen years old."

"Accustom yourself to it. I mean to keep right on winking at you."

They sat side by side that way, touching from shoulder to knee, happily eating their humble meal, making light conversation in the quiet of evening. It was a fine way to spend a quarter hour.

"What have you left to do in your garden tonight?" Robbie asked him after they'd finished their meal.

"It's not *my* garden," he said with a smile. "Not really."

"You designed and built it. You made it beautiful, and beautiful in a way that lasts. That's owing to you, and that gives you a claim to it that can't be taken away." It was, quite possibly, one of the kindest things a woman had ever said to him.

"If that's true, then I have fine gardens all over the kingdom."

"Quite the landowner, you are." Robbie rose, her smile seemingly permanent. She turned to face him. "What's left to be done in your garden tonight?"

He stood as well. "Only putting away my tools."

"Can I help you with that?"

Even if she couldn't have done a single thing to assist in what little remained to be done, he'd have told her she could. Howard hadn't ever been one who fell to pieces when separated from people he missed, but he had a sense of that changing, of his need for Robbie MacGregor, growing stronger by the day.

He didn't know how much of her company he had left to enjoy, but he meant to claim every bit of it she'd allow.

He walked with her hand in his own back into the garden he was building, pleased as plums at the approval he saw in her eyes when she looked at all he'd accomplished.

"Would you mind too terribly if I wandered down this way in the evenings?" Robbie asked. "I'll bring you your supper and help you with what I can."

"Having you here to end my day would be the greatest Christmastime present I can think of."

She smiled at him. "You'll remember it's not actually Christmas."

"And yet I'm certain I'll look back on this not-actually-Christmas celebration as my favorite Yuletide of all."

Quite without warning, Robbie pressed a kiss to his stubbled cheek. "So will I."

Chapter Fourteen

Lady Jonquil allowed Robbie to visit the circular sitting room each day and watch Howard as he worked below. Robbie didn't remain for hours on end but did take advantage of a moment here and there. And, to her relief, Lady Jonquil didn't tease her about it.

At the end of each day, when Adam was spending time with his host and hostess, Robbie slipped out to the garden corner to visit with Howard and talk about how his work was progressing. A handful of days since she'd first done so, she made her evening walk outside, and Howard was next to the garden wall, waiting for her.

He smiled as she approached. Her heart flipped around as it did whenever she found herself in his company.

"This is quickly becoming my favorite time of day," he said. For someone who'd been so gruff when she'd first met him, Howard was proving rather romantic in his sensibilities.

She walked beside him and looked around. "The wall must be nearly finished."

"There are only a few places here and there that still need attention," he said. "But the bulk of the work is done. Lord Jonquil means to take a look tomorrow and give his approval or disapproval."

"I can't imagine he would disapprove."

Her words didn't seem to fully reassure Howard. "His is a generous nature, and I worry he'll say he is pleased when, in reality, he isn't entirely. I hope not. I need him to be ecstatic."

She slipped her arm through his, continuing to walk at his side. Howard had told her of his hopes for this job. He'd explained that if someone with the influence and standing of Lord Jonquil bragged about his new garden to his friends or recommended that others employ Howard for similar projects, it'd be a boon to his livelihood. It was little wonder he'd been so concerned when he'd first learned a young boy with the potential to cause mischief was on the premises.

"I think even an ungenerous person must look at your work thus far and be pleased with it."

He smiled at her, an expression that came easily and frequent of late. "The rowan arrived today. I mean to plant it tomorrow."

"I'd love to see it," she said.

They walked together back along the side of the wall and into the opening that would hold the gate. That placed them inside the newly enclosed garden wall. The bricks he'd been laying the day she'd helped turn over soil were now small retaining walls. The space didn't yet have its stone walkway or benches or even any of the flowers or shrubs. But leaning a little against the long-established wall on one side of the garden was a small tree, its root ball wrapped in heavy burlap.

"Do trees always arrive this way?" she asked.

"If those doing the hauling know what they're doing, yes. If they are moved about without any care given to the roots, the trees are more likely to die."

"It seems even stately trees need protecting."

Howard nodded. "Trees and shrubs and such can be very sturdy, but they need to be given some care. They need us to know what they require and what'll help them thrive."

Robbie slipped her hands free of his and moved to the area of the garden where she remembered the tree was meant to be planted. She stood there, her gaze moving from the yet-to-be-planted tree to the spot where it was meant to go.

"It looks a wee bit small for the space just now," she said. "Is it a young tree, then, that still has a fair lot of growing to do?"

"Precisely. It will grow into the space it has been given, which is why I want to make certain it is planted well and has everything it needs to become what it can be."

"It seems to me designing and planting a garden is nae entirely unlike being a nursemaid. We look after the children in our care, make ourselves aware of what they need and what it is that helps them thrive. By the time they leave our care, our hope is that we've placed them on the path and in the place where they have what they need to become the people they can become."

Howard walked slowly over to her, his eyes studying her face. He set his hands on her arms, then slid them slowly until his fingers threaded through hers. "Perhaps that is why you so quickly and easily learned to work in a garden."

"I've had a very good teacher."

A sly little smile began pulling at his lips.

She couldn't help herself and added, "The gardener at Falstone Castle."

Howard laughed out loud, his head tilting backward and his eyes dancing about.

She didn't consider herself an unhappy or somber person, but it had been a long time since she'd known someone who genuinely laughed with her and did so regularly. She loved that about him. She loved a lot of things about him.

From the direction of the wall opening came a small authoritative voice. "Nurse Robbie, I need to speak with you."

She looked in that direction, as did Howard. There was no question who had spoken, and yet it was still odd to see Adam there. He hadn't yet ventured near the garden. Perhaps he knew stonework could be dangerous. Perhaps it was yet another indicator that he struggled with his acceptance of Howard.

"What is it you need to say?" Robbie moved closer to him.

Before Adam could answer, Pooka came bursting past him, yelping and barking excitedly and running an energetic circle around the little boy. Adam sighed, his expression one of exasperation. When they'd first come to Brier Hill, he'd been afraid of the tiny dog. Lord Jonquil had taken time to show him how to interact with the rambunctious little thing, to help him not be afraid.

"Hush, Pooka," he said in ringing tones of authority. The dog stopped circling and planted itself directly in front of Adam, looking up at him, wagging its little tail eagerly. To Robbie, Adam said, "He thinks I want only to play with him. He doesn't know that I have important things to do."

Her wee Adam sounded more grown-up with each passing day. Too grown-up at times.

"Well, he'll sit there and watch you while you talk," Robbie said. "Then you needn't be prevented from telling me what you came to say."

Adam nodded quite regally. "I wish to plan a party."

A feather might have knocked Robbie clear over at that declaration. "A party?" She must've heard him wrong.

Another quick nod. "We had our Christmas celebration. After Christmas is Twelfth Night. I think we should have a Twelfth Night celebration. I think Lord and Lady Jonquil would enjoy it." The last bit was spoken with hesitancy and a little uncertainty.

"I suspect they would fancy a Twelfth Night party," Robbie said. "But *you* aren't fond of gatherings or parties."

"Neither was my father, but he still held them. He planned balls and gatherings and dinners because Mother liked them. Ladies like those things, I think."

"You want to plan this one because Lady Jonquil would like it?"

Another quick nod. This time his brow pulled in a combination of embarrassment and uncertainty. He had all but perfected the unwaveringly confident mien that his father had so often exhibited, but Adam couldn't hide the fact that, at his heart, he was still a little boy.

"Twelfth Night comes nearly twelve days after Christmas," Robbie reminded him. "By the time we reach eleven days after *our* Christmas celebration, you'll nae be here any longer." She'd given him the explanation so he'd understand the obstacle he faced. But speaking it aloud drove home just how short *her* time at Brier Hill was. She would be here less than a fortnight longer. Less than a fortnight to walk with Howard and talk with him.

Howard must've sensed her distress. He stepped up beside her and silently took her hand, as he'd done in the pony cart several days earlier.

"We did not celebrate Christmas on Christmas Day," Adam said. "Can't we have our Twelfth Night celebration whenever we want? It isn't a real one, after all."

Howard entered the conversation for the first time. "That is a delightful idea, Your Grace. And I think, as an added special gift to Lord and Lady Jonquil, the three of us could do the work planning it. Lady Jonquil has looked a bit tired of late, as soon-to-be mothers often do. A little extra rest would be good for her."

Adam watched him with a mixture of uncertainty and distrust. Spending some time with Howard might help Adam overcome his worries about him. On the other hand, it might simply solidify his suspicions that Howard was taking her away.

"I think you've a good plan," Robbie said, hoping she was encouraging the right approach. "Which aspects of the celebration ought we to include?"

Adam shrugged, a little of his enthusiasm having drained from him. "I don't know very much about it. Father and I had cake on Twelfth Night, but nothing more than that."

The old duke hadn't been one for celebrations, except when he thought they might bring his wife home.

"Twelfth Night was quite a raucous time at my house growing up," Howard said. "I can tell you all about it."

All of a sudden, Adam's posture turned unyielding and ramrod straight. "You can tell Nurse Robbie, and she can tell me. I don't need *you* to tell me anything." With that, he spun around, and rather than walk away with palpable dignity, he ran. Pooka ran after him.

"I hadn't meant to upset the boy," Howard said.

"I do nae think you did." She leaned her head against his shoulder. Without hesitation he slipped his arms around her and held her in a tender embrace. He'd held her many times since their rainy-afternoon encounter. The experience usually sent her heart fluttering and her mind spinning. This time it brought a sense of peace and calm.

"I think he realizes my time as his nursemaid is drawing to an end. He doesn't know a great deal of the world, but he's a bright boy. And while he does a fine job of appearing as if nothing bothers him or hurts or scares him, underneath that mask, he's terrified."

"And anything or anyone who contributes to his worries of losing you gets pushed away."

"Aye."

Howard bent his head enough to whisper into her ear, "He loves you, Robbie—it is not a difficult thing to do—but he feels torn."

"I do as well," she whispered.

He pressed a kiss to her temple. "I know."

She lifted her chin to look into his deep, earth-colored eyes, so full of compassion and concern. "And do you also know that I love you?"

"I've had my suspicions, but it's nice to hear it. Does my heart a whole heap of good." He kissed the tip of her nose. "I love you too. Amazing how quickly and fully that happened, i'n' it?"

"Wonderfully amazing."

Howard bent a bit more, enough to press his lips to hers. The kiss was delicate and faint and yet still heart-stopping. She brushed her fingers over the stubble on his jaw, reveling in the simple pleasure of being near enough to touch him.

"We may not have the answers just now, Robbie, but I'm a patient man. And I'm not easily discouraged. We'll sort an answer. I know we will."

Chapter Fifteen

Howard was in the midst of digging a hole for the rowan tree the next day when Adam and Lord Jonquil arrived there. He paused in his work and waited to hear what it was they needed. Adam was the first to offer an explanation.

"Lord Jonquil is going to help with our Twelfth Night party. I thought it best that he participate since he knows where everything is and he will know what Lady Jonquil would like to do."

"Wise," Howard said.

Adam gave a very regal dip of his head. He was the most duke-like eight-year-old Howard had ever met. Once the boy was grown, he would be formidable.

Lord Jonquil stepped a little closer and, lowering his voice, said, "I'll make certain the boy doesn't disrupt your work overly much or put himself in danger, but I do think Miss MacGregor would be less anxious if Adam were more at ease with you."

That was true as the day was long. His voice at conversational volume, Howard said, "If the two of you don't mind helping a bit here, we could discuss our plans as we work."

Adam looked around the garden doubtfully.

"We just finished a little jaunt around the area," Lord Jonquil said. He motioned to his clothes, simple and made of the rough-spun fabric generally worn by laborers. "So we're quite well dressed for the undertaking."

Howard gave Adam a quick look-over. The boy's clothing up until now had been quite formal, no doubt in deference to his rank. But he was, just now, dressed quite casually. The coat he wore, Howard would guess, actually belonged to one of the servants at Brier Hill. It fit him overly large, and the sleeves were rolled up, but it was too small to have been Lord Jonquil's. His collar lay open.

His trousers were a bit dirty, his hair a bit mussed. The black sash he'd been gifted at their Christmas celebration was tied about his middle, visible beneath the front edge of his coat. It was good for young ones to be able to get a little messy now and then. It was good for people, old and young alike, to spend a little time with the earth.

Howard motioned with his shovel toward a pallet of dirt in which were a few small flowering shrubs. "Those are holly bushes. They're to be planted two in that section"—he motioned to his right—"and one in that section." He motioned to the left and just a touch behind himself. "I'll give you a mark where they're supposed to go. If you'd start digging holes, that would help a lot."

Lord Jonquil didn't need to be asked twice. Howard had had enough conversations with the gentleman to know he was well-versed in the art of cultivating plants and had a love of doing so.

He abandoned, for the moment, the hole he was digging for the rowan tree and moved to the sections of the garden where the hollies were being planted. With the blade of his shovel, he marked very clear *x*'s in the moist soil to tell his unexpected helpers where to dig.

Lord Jonquil picked out digging implements for the two of them, doing a fine job of selecting the right ones for their relative sizes and abilities. The gentleman took to the work immediately. Adam was far more hesitant.

"The wonderful thing about digging," Howard said, "is it's a simple thing to learn. You keep your back firm and strong, bend your knees, put your shoulders into it, and pull out the soil."

Adam nodded but with lingering uncertainty. Howard suspected the boy wouldn't appreciate being analyzed as he tried his hand at something new, so he put his attention to his own digging, following his own instructions. He could hear the other two having a discussion. Lord Jonquil had ample praise for his little helper. Adam was full of questions. The boy didn't seem to know whether he liked the feel of damp soil under his feet. He outright said he didn't want any on his hands.

Lord Jonquil laughed and said he'd always liked getting dirty. That was another odd thing about this lord. All the Quality Howard had interacted with appreciated gardens for their beauty or their abundance, but few had any interest in doing the work themselves.

Once Adam was focused on his digging efforts, Howard opened up the topic they'd come to the garden to discuss. "Has your Nurse Robbie talked to you of the Twelfth Night traditions I shared with her?" he asked.

"She told me it wasn't fair to require her to make a list when I could just ask you." That didn't seem to meet with the young duke's approval. "She was very stubborn about it."

Howard thought he understood. Just as Lord Jonquil had brought the boy to the garden in an attempt to broker peace between him and the man he likely feared was stealing his nursemaid away, Robbie was attempting to nudge them toward something of a ceasefire as well.

"I'm happy enough to share with you what we did when I was child," Howard said.

Adam looked to Lord Jonquil, a question clear in his expression. Lord Jonquil gave him silent encouragement to push forward.

"What is a person meant to do on Twelfth Night?" Adam asked but didn't deign to look at Howard.

"The wonderful thing about Twelfth Night," Howard said, "is that the entire purpose is enjoyment. It is the final day of the Christmas season, the last evening of revelry before the new year begins. Twelfth Night is a night for games, merriment, and music. You mentioned you and your father ate cake on Twelfth Night. Cake is a must. This was, in fact, the only day in the entire year when my family ate cake."

Adam's eyes pulled a little wide. "The only one?"

Howard didn't think this the appropriate time to discuss the realities of poverty, so he wrapped the fact up in a bit of fancy paper. "That made Twelfth Night cake extra special."

Adam looked to his digging partner. "Did you have cake on Twelfth Night?"

"We most certainly did," Lord Jonquil said. "And every year I wished ever so hard that I would be the one to find the bean."

Adam's confusion grew twentyfold.

"The cake you ate with your father didn't have a bean?" Howard asked him.

"I've never heard of beans in a cake." Adam had a bit of mud on his hand and eyed it with fiercely drawn brows.

Lord Jonquil mimed flinging the mud off his fingers. Adam did his utmost to manage it. Howard decided to push forward with his explanation of beans in Twelfth Night cakes in an effort to prevent his delighted amusement from showing. Adam had shown himself sensitive about such things.

"Beans in cakes is one of the most specific Twelfth Night traditions." Howard leaned against the upturned handle of his shovel. "On Twelfth Night, the cake is baked with a bean inside. I have heard some families use dried peas, but ours always used a bean."

"As did ours," Lord Jonquil said, continuing to dig with apparent enjoyment.

Adam was watching Howard with great interest.

"While we certainly enjoyed our cake, its purpose is not to be a treat. Its purpose is the bean." Howard allowed all the excitement he'd felt as a child on Twelfth Night to enter his voice, hoping to fill Adam with a little bit of it. "You see, Your Grace, the person who finds the bean is crowned king or queen for the night."

His eyes pulled wider. The child did a very good job of hiding his thoughts and feelings, but Howard was getting better at understanding what he kept tucked away.

"As the ruling monarch, that person chooses how the night is spent. The monarch of the evening decides which games to play, which songs to sing, which vignettes should be undertaken."

"What's that?" The tiniest bit of breathlessness entered his voice.

"It is another Twelfth Night diversion," Lord Jonquil answered. "The participants are given a scene or an idea or a story that they are challenged with presenting. They choose poses meant to evoke the idea of it. If the monarch of the evening so wishes, and such things are at hand, they might even piece together costumes of some sort."

"What is the purpose of vignettes?" Adam asked him.

"Those seeing them are challenged with determining what is being portrayed."

"I understand about challenges," Adam said. "My father told me that sometimes we have to do things that are difficult, but it's the difficulty that gives us pride in accomplishing it."

"I said it before, Your Grace," Howard said, "your father was clearly very wise."

The tiniest of smiles touched the little boy's scarred face. The moment gifted Howard with an insight into this little one whom he was meant to gain the confidence of. Adam loved his father and was proud of him. He was likely as protective of his father's memory as he was of his nursemaid's present. Speaking highly of Robbie would not be difficult at all, but it would make a difference. He needed to not merely speak well of the late duke but also allow *Adam* to speak well of him.

Howard returned to his digging, suspecting Adam would be more comfortable if he felt his audience wasn't staring at him.

"Did your father have any favorite tales or stories?" Howard asked. "Perhaps we could use those as vignettes to present in our Twelfth Night celebration."

"If the monarch of the night wants to," Adam said.

Howard gave him an approving and impressed smile. "Sorted that rather quickly, didn't you?"

"I'm very clever." The declaration was made very matter-of-factly.

"Clever, yes, but you're not doing nearly as much digging as I am," Lord Jonquil said with a laugh.

Adam grinned at him. The effect pulled fiercely at Howard's heart. In that moment he could see the child that lingered behind the heavy heart. There was a naturalness to his smile that told anyone who saw it how joyful and soft a heart lay at the core of this very guarded child. What would become of him if he lost Robbie?

Howard appreciated his beloved's conundrum. He understood that she cared for Adam and worried about him. He fully appreciated that. Stepping away from the boy must feel very much like stepping away from a child of her own. Howard had assumed that was at the heart of what she was struggling with.

Now he knew better.

This was a child in crisis. He would not simply be sad without Robbie in his life; he would be lost. The glimmer of hopefulness and tenderness that still remained in him would fade away until it was gone. It was little wonder she had clung so much to Howard's use of the word *hope*. Adam needed it desperately. Robbie couldn't feel hopeful herself unless she knew there was reason to believe Adam felt it too.

They had quite a dilemma on their hands.

Adam had resumed his digging. He was small, but he was strong and determined. "What else happens on Twelfth Night?"

"Well, it is also traditional for the tenants of a fine estate to visit the home of the master and mistress who own it." Howard did his digging as he talked. "They often sing songs, and in exchange, the master and mistress give them drink and food. They are often given coins and other acknowledgments of the season. In some areas of the country, trees are wassailed."

Again, Adam looked at him with widening eyes. "How does one wassail a tree?"

"Very carefully," Lord Jonquil said.

In addition to discovering that his current employer enjoyed nature, Howard had very quickly realized the gentleman was exceptionally funny.

"Bread is soaked in wassail," Howard explained, "and then tossed into the trees. It provides sustenance for the birds. Superstition claims it also brings good luck and an ample harvest."

"Could we wassail this tree?" Adam pointed to the rowan Howard hoped to have planted by day's end.

"I don't see why not," he said.

Adam turned to Lord Jonquil, eagerness in his expression. "If we wassail your new tree, it will bring you good luck with your new garden. And you and Lady Jonquil can sit in it and be happy. And when your baby is here at Brier Hill, all of you can visit the garden."

"I think that is an excellent idea," Lord Jonquil said. "With one change."

A portion of the boy's walls immediately began reenforcing themselves.

"You have to promise you will come visit this garden too," Lord Jonquil said, resting a hand on Adam's shoulder.

The boy's gaze dropped to the dirt at his feet. "This isn't my house. I'm not part of your family."

Lord Jonquil knelt in front of him, setting his hands on the boy's arms. "Family is who you choose, Adam Boyce. Julia and I, we have chosen you. That makes you family to us. When you are away at school, we will be family. When we travel to Nottinghamshire to see our parents, you and Lady Jonquil and I will be family. Every time you visit us, be it here or anywhere else, we will be family."

"I would like that," he said with a little break in his voice.

"And your dear Nurse Robbie, she is your family, no matter where she is and no matter where you are. You are family because you choose to be."

Howard heard the little boy take a deep, trembling breath, the sort one took when trying not to cry.

"Family doesn't stop being family just because they aren't together," Adam said.

Lord Jonquil gently touched his sweet, scarred face. "That is exactly right."

Adam smiled, the expression shaky but content.

"If Mr. Simpkin finds the bean on Twelfth Night," Adam said, "do you think he'll make everyone dig holes?"

Lord Jonquil didn't appear to know what to make of that at first. Howard himself wasn't certain what had inspired the question. Then the most amazing thing happened. Adam's mouth, only moments earlier pulled down in sorrow and grief, slowly tugged upward into the most mischievous smile he had just about ever seen.

A laugh burst from Howard. Lord Jonquil joined him an instant later. While Adam didn't actually laugh, he grinned. Lord Jonquil stood once more and ruffled the boy's hair, sending his black waves into utter chaos. Adam didn't seem to care; he simply took up his shovel once more and set back to work.

"The most important thing to sort for our Twelfth Night celebration," Howard said, "is what our womenfolk would most enjoy. If we can bring them cheer, they'll be quite pleased with the lot of us."

"There is a life lesson in that for the two of us, Adam," Lord Jonquil said, assuming a demeanor so serious, no one could possibly take it seriously. "Anytime you can make the women you care about happy, that's a fine thing."

"Lady Jonquil likes ginger biscuits," Adam said.

"She does indeed."

"What does your Nurse Robbie like most to eat, do you suppose?" Howard asked Adam, suspecting he enjoyed talking about the woman who'd been his sure foundation for so long.

"She likes plum pudding."

Howard tucked that bit of information away.

"I suspect we can convince Cook to make more ginger biscuits and some plum pudding," Lord Jonquil said. "And I believe we can manage to have a Twelfth Night cake."

"Will it have a bean in it?" Adam asked.

"Of course."

Adam was digging in earnest now. He'd managed to find his rhythm with the work. Perhaps the boy would come over from the house and help every day. Howard could make some headway in earning the boy's good opinion. Perhaps that would also grant him even more time with Robbie. Dear, darling Robbie.

"There is but one more thing to decide," Lord Jonquil said.

"What's that?" Howard asked.

"What we ought to sort is a means of making a very impressive showing for ourselves just now. You see, we are being watched."

Howard glanced around, as did Adam. There was no one about.

"The window high on the back of the house," Lord Jonquil said. "There are two womenfolk standing there just now, watching us."

Howard looked up. Sure enough, Lady Jonquil and Robbie both stood at the window, looking down on them.

"We could do a vignette," Adam suggested.

"Excellent." Lord Jonquil looked excited. "I suggest we select something that makes the three of us look incredibly impressive."

"What about Charon?" Adam asked.

"The ferryman on the river Styx?" Lord Jonquil nodded his approval. "Have you a fondness for the Greek myths?"

Adam shrugged. "I think about them sometimes. I don't really know why. They feel . . . important."

"They are rather fascinating," Lord Jonquil said.

"And rather perfect for our purposes," Howard said.

Thus began a thorough but very quick discussion of how to create their little vignette of Charon punting two poor souls to the underworld. They needed but a few moments to sort the particulars.

On a signal from Adam, they rushed to assume their poses, the young duke portraying the ferryman and his adult companions quite dramatically portraying the unwitting passengers. Howard looked up at the window. His dear Robbie was laughing quite heartily.

"I think we made them feel happy," Adam said. "Anytime a man can do something to make the women he cares about happy, that is a fine thing."

"A fine thing indeed," Howard said.

Chapter Sixteen

Preparations began in earnest the day before the planned Twelfth Night celebration. Somehow, the planners had managed to keep their scheme a secret from Lady Jonquil. Robbie had never before considered herself a mischief-maker, and she was rather enjoying having a scheme to participate in. And a Christmastime scheme seemed to her the very best sort.

It was midmorning, and Robbie, Adam, and Lord Jonquil had plans to ride out in the pony cart to gather a bit of greenery for making a Twelfth Night crown. Howard wasn't able to join them. In fact, he was just then returning from the village with the pony cart, having made a quick jaunt there for a few supplies he needed.

"We should find branches like the ones on the mantel," Adam said, watching the cart approach with an eagerness that was unusual for him—at least, it had been before coming to Brier Hill. "They are very Christmassy."

"Christmassy things are rather wonderful, aren't they?" Lord Jonquil observed. He was holding Adam's hand, something the boy had permitted so few people to do. Even Robbie wasn't permitted to do so any longer.

"Do you like Christmassy things, Nurse Robbie?" Adam asked.

I'll look back on this not-actually-Christmas celebration as my favorite Yuletide of all. Robbie's heart leaped about as Howard's declaration echoed in her mind. "I very much like Christmassy things."

The pony cart reached the spot where they were waiting. Howard doffed his hat to all of them but offered a subtle wink to Robbie. He truly did mean to keep doing that, it seemed. She didn't mind in the least.

He alighted and placed himself at the pony's head. "I've kept the beast to a sedate pace, Lord Jonquil. The animal should have vigor enough for your greenery gathering."

"You have our thanks. Ours is a very important mission."

"I know it is."

Lord Jonquil lifted Adam up into the cart, then climbed up onto the bench and took up the reins. "I assume you'd not object to seeing Miss MacGregor settled on the bench."

"No objection in the least." Howard grinned broadly.

With Lord Jonquil in control of the pony, Howard made his way to where Robbie stood. Her heart flipped about more and more each time she saw him.

"I wish I could wander about with you, looking for greenery," he said.

"I know you've work to do. And we'll see you this evening when we undertake preparations in earnest."

His eyes moved to Adam. "As I've promised, Your Grace."

Adam offered a very proper and undeniably regal nod.

Howard looked to her once more. "Until this evening, Robbie." He held out a small fabric-wrapped bundle. "And, until then, here's something to make your day brighter."

He'd brought her a gift? "What is it?"

"Something I'm told you're fond of." Another wink. "Open it as you're driving out, enjoying nature." He handed her up onto the pony bench.

"Thank you," she said. "For whatever this is."

"You're quite welcome."

A moment later, the cart was on its way. Robbie watched Howard for as long as she could see him. How quickly her heart had grown fully attached to him.

"What did Mr. Simpkin give you?" Adam asked.

"I don't know. I haven't opened it yet."

"He said you were supposed to open it while we were driving out in search of greenery." Adam spoke quite seriously. "It would be ridiculous not to open it."

Robbie held back her amusement. "I'd not wish to be ridiculous." She untied the bit of twine holding the fabric together, the bundle sitting on her lap. She peeled back the fabric to reveal inside a small plum pudding. "Oh, lovely."

Adam's eyes grew wide. "He remembered."

"Remembered what?"

"I told him, when we were digging in the garden, that you liked plum pudding. And he remembered."

Her dear, darling Howard. He remembered.

Howard finished his work for the day as quickly as he could manage, then proceeded directly to the guest bedchamber where Adam and Robbie were staying during their time at Brier Hill. He had promised to help the little boy and his nursemaid finish their preparations.

He paused on the threshold, watching Robbie interact with her little duke. She offered patient encouragement as Adam lay on the floor, doing his utmost to keep a toy top spinning. He wanted it to spin far longer than it was. Robbie assured him he would get the knack of it soon enough.

Keeping quiet so he wouldn't disrupt them, Howard slipped inside the room. He'd brought some supplies with him for making a shovegroat board. The coachman had given him a discarded bit of wood. Growing up, Howard and his brothers and sisters had played shovegroat in the dirt. It worked far better on something smooth like wood. And he suspected Adam would enjoy making the game board.

He didn't set down his supplies quite as quietly as he'd walked, and that brought attention to him. He smiled at Robbie. He then dipped his head to Adam. He never quite knew how to interact with the boy. He was a duke, yes, but he was also a child.

"I thought of a game we might enjoy playing on Twelfth Night," Howard said.

"If the king or queen decides to." Adam had latched on to that aspect of the celebration very quickly.

"Of course," Howard said. "But, in case our monarch does decide on this game, we need to prepare the shovegroat board."

Adam shifted his position from lying on his stomach to sitting on the floor. He looked at Howard with his characteristic authoritative curiosity. "What is a shovegroat board?"

"It is simple, really. I've already sanded the wood so it's smooth. There will be horizontal lines painted across the board at an equal distance from each other with numbers beneath each line. Those numbers are how the game is scored."

Adam twisted and got on his feet, crossed to where Howard was, and eyed the blank board. "There aren't any numbers or lines."

Howard nodded his acknowledgment. "We need to do that part. Since we planned to do our Twelfth Night preparations this evening, I thought we could paint ourselves a shovegroat board too."

"I don't want to do that," Adam said. He tended to tuck himself behind forcefulness when he was unsure about something.

"I'm certain Mr. Simpkin'll show you how," Robbie said.

"What about the Twelfth Night crown?" Adam asked. "We were supposed to make that tonight."

"There'll be time enough," Robbie said. "We needn't make any special decorations or gather presents. Twelfth Night does nae call for any. It is, in fact, traditionally when the Christmas greenery is removed."

That angled Adam's dark brow with disappointment. "Do we have to take it down? Since it isn't the real Twelfth Night?"

Robbie set a hand on his shoulder. "Would you like to have the greenery remain?"

In a voice a bit smaller and a little less certain than he often employed, Adam said, "I like it. It smells nice."

"Evergreens and herbs and flowers smell divine," Howard said. "It's one of the things I like best about gardens."

"Maybe that is why Lord Jonquil likes gardens," Adam said.

"Perhaps," Robbie said. "Gardens are very peaceful. I think many people like them because they help when we're sad or overwhelmed or sorrowing."

Adam seemed to ponder that.

"What would you like to tackle first?" Howard asked. "We can begin with the crown, or we can begin with the shovegroat board."

"Can Nurse Robbie help us with the board?"

"Of course," he said. "I don't think either of us would want to do something she wasn't part of."

Adam didn't seem to know whether he approved of that sentiment. Howard hoped he was making some headway in convincing the child to trust him and accept that he hoped to be part of Robbie's life even as she was becoming less a part of Adam's.

The boy climbed into the armchair beside the side table where they would be undertaking their tasks. He was drowned by its size, and yet, somehow, he didn't seem out of place. He was an odd combination of child and grown-up.

Howard offered Robbie the other chair. At first, she seemed as if she meant to object, but he did not relent.

"I spend my days standing and walking about," he said. "I like it. Given the choice between sitting and being on my feet, I always choose the latter."

That seemed to convince her, and she sat.

"These are the tools we're going to need to make our shovegroat board." He slid over to them the lead pencil, paint, and paintbrush he'd brought. "Are you familiar with shovegroat, Robbie?"

She nodded. "A family I worked for ten years ago or more enjoyed the game. You chose well."

He tossed her a mischievous look. "I know."

Her eyes met his, a warmth filling them. "It seems we both have good taste."

"Can the board have more than just lines and numbers?" Adam asked, studying the blank surface.

"It surely can," Howard said.

"We should paint holly and ivy on it," Adam said. "Since it is for our Twelfth Night celebration."

"A bonnie idea, that," Robbie said.

She helped Adam undertake the task of creating the shovegroat board. He was quite happy to draw the lines on the board using the pencil but initially resisted the task of painting until Robbie made him do it grudgingly. Howard hoped that someday Adam would find enough confidence in himself to take up new and unfamiliar things more willingly.

It was a pleasant half an hour creating the board. He felt certain that if any of the adults were crowned monarch of Twelfth Night, he or she would choose this game so their little duke could enjoy the fruits of his labor.

Once the board was finished, Robbie set it very carefully atop the tallboy, where it could safely dry. She then gathered the supplies for making the crown, the greenery they'd gathered with Lord Jonquil that afternoon. Pressing work in the garden had prevented Howard from accompanying her in the task, and his heart had dropped completely into his boots as searing disappointment had filled his chest at losing the opportunity for a few extra minutes with her. He couldn't remember the last time he had felt discontented while surrounded by nature.

"You managed to procure some twine," he said as Robbie set the supplies on the table.

"Lord Jonquil and I stole it," Adam said. "We pretended we were highwaymen. We had to be very stealthy to get it. And I wore my black sash."

It was good to hear the boy talk about being imaginative and a touch silly. The look of relief on Robbie's face told Howard she, too, was grateful to see her dear duke being a child.

Howard gently curved the evergreen branches, holding them together while Robbie and Adam took turns using twine to tie them. Once they created a full circle of branches, the task turned to beautifying the thing.

"I don't know where this is supposed to go," Adam said, holding up a sprig of rosemary.

"There isn't a proper place," Howard said. "You can put it wherever you'd like."

Adam shook his head. "There are proper ways to do things."

"The proper way, in this instance," Robbie said, "is however the person creating the crown chooses."

"I don't think that should be a proper way. Someone might make a mistake and he wouldn't even know."

Howard had realized fairly early on that Adam was a bit shy. He was beginning to realize this tiny duke was quite a lot anxious.

Robbie showed herself adept at reassuring him while not allowing him to rest on his laurels. She helped him have confidence without encouraging him to be arrogant or overbearing. Howard doubted many people could manage the balance.

Ever since Robbie had explained her dilemma, Howard had assumed their difficulty was finding a way to convince Adam that all would be well if Robbie left. He'd begun to fear he had misunderstood the problem. Rather than preparing Adam for Robbie's departure, it might very well be that Howard needed to wrap *his* mind around the necessity of her remaining.

Chapter Seventeen

Robbie used to change Adam into his nightclothes and tuck him into his bed after warming it with a warming pan. She used to sing to him every night, almost always the song about the wee boy as small as a thistle. He'd not asked that of her since returning from Harrow. He prepared himself for bed, tucked himself in, and laid down to sleep without music or hugs or the slew of questions he used to ask.

Mothers must experience this as well: their children growing up, and being left trying to determine what their changing role is.

Robbie pulled the door closed as she stepped out into the corridor. Howard was waiting there. She'd not even needed to ask him to.

He took her hand and kissed it, very much the way a gallant gentleman would with the hand of a fine lady.

"Do you have to rush out, or can you jaw with me a spell?" Robbie asked.

"I've all the time in the world for you." He often said tender things like that. She loved that about him.

They wandered a bit down the corridor, farther from the room where Adam would soon be asleep.

"A few days ago," Robbie said, "Lady Jonquil wrote to the Duchess of Kielder asking that Adam visit them during every term break he is able to do so. The castle is a lonely place for him. Here, at Brier Hill, he is more than merely welcomed; he's . . ." She searched about for the right word.

"Family," Howard supplied. "I've seen that myself."

"A response from the duchess arrived today."

They stopped walking, and Howard, without hesitation, set his arms around her.

"She did agree that Adam could come visit Lord and Lady Jonquil," Robbie said.

"Why does that not sound like the good news it ought to be?"

Every inch of her felt heavy and tired. "She pushed back at the idea of him coming here on every term break or even on most of them. She insists he needs to spend time at Falstone Castle so he doesn't grow distant from it and the responsibilities he has there. She says the people there and those he will oversee when he is of age need to know him and be known to him."

Howard's expression was hesitant, as was his tone when he spoke. "I don't think Her Grace is entirely wrong on that score."

Robbie nodded. "I know. But it breaks my heart that Adam is, once again, being sacrificed for the sake of the title he inherited far too young."

Howard kissed her temple, softly and tenderly.

"The duchess also said she would be looking to hire a governess," Robbie said.

"Oh, dearest." No matter that this wasn't a surprise, Howard seemed to realize that the inarguable proof of her time at Falstone Castle coming to a close had dealt her a blow.

"Lady Jonquil will write back and offer to help with the search. She hopes that, in light of the duchess's indifferent approach to Adam and the running of the castle, the duchess might allow Lady Jonquil to choose a governess. Then she can find someone who'll understand Adam and be kind to him, someone who'll bring him to Brier Hill as often as his mother will allow."

"That doesn't address your situation though," Howard said. "Even the kindest of governesses will not be *you*. That will be difficult for you and your little duke."

"I'll be so far away from him."

"Not if you accept Lord and Lady Jonquil's offer to be a nursemaid for their coming arrival," Howard said. "You'd be a day's journey from Falstone Forest. You'd be here whenever he was permitted to visit. You'd still see him."

She looked up into those beloved eyes, her heart breaking anew. "But I wouldn't see you. You can't stay here."

He brushed his thumb over her cheek. "I do have to go where I find work. That requires me to travel."

"I know." She lowered her gaze, her heart too heavy for meeting his eyes any longer.

"How long do you suspect Adam will need you to be nearby while the ground beneath him solidifies?"

She hadn't thought of it in quite that way. Over time, Adam would grow more independent. He would be used to living at Harrow and traveling back at term breaks. He would adjust to his new governess. While he would never stop mourning the death of his father, that loss would, with time, be less new and less fresh.

"I'm nae certain how long he'll need," she said. "He might prove more adaptable than he seems now. He might, on the other hand, need a year or two."

Howard kissed her lightly on the lips. "I have told you before that I am patient. I'm in earnest, Robbie. If we need to wait two years while your precious Adam gains his footing and while your heart is reassured of his well-being, then I can wait. To be with you, I can wait as long as is required."

She wrapped her arms around him. "I wish we didn't have to."

"So do I, Robbie. So do I."

Adam stood in the doorway of his bedchamber, a whirlwind of thoughts and feelings twisting him about. He understood most of what Nurse Robbie and Mr. Simpkin were saying, but he couldn't entirely make sense of it. He needed help sorting it all.

Careful to be very quiet, he slipped down the corridor in the opposite direction of Nurse Robbie and directly to Lady Jonquil's bedchamber. He wasn't certain she would be in there. Eight-year-old boys, after all, went to bed much earlier than grown-up ladies.

Relief wrapped around his heart when he saw her sitting on her bed and reading a book. He tiptoed closer, unsure how to begin. He knew she wouldn't be upset to see him—she never was—but she might not approve of him eavesdropping on Nurse Robbie's conversation.

"Lady Jonquil?" He didn't like when the words he said came out small. He was already too little for everything he was supposed to do—be a duke, look after the castle, go to school—*sounding* too little only meant people would laugh at him more.

She looked over at him. Lady Jonquil always smiled when she saw him. He liked that. "Adam. I thought you would be in bed already."

"I was," he admitted. "But I heard something that confused me. And worried me. And I needed to . . . I wanted to ask you about it."

She patted the bed beside her. "Climb up, sweeting, and tell me what you heard."

He didn't hesitate. His long nightshirt gave him a bit of trouble, but he managed to position himself right next to her.

Lady Jonquil set her book aside and turned so she was facing him. "What was it you heard?"

"Nurse Robbie said to Mr. Simpkin that she won't be my nurse anymore."

"With you not living at the castle all the time any longer and you being eight years old now, with no younger children there for her to look after, she would have nothing to do."

He didn't like that explanation. "She said my mother said I'm to have a governess."

Lady Jonquil nodded. "That is usually what happens next."

"Why could not Nurse Robbie be my governess? It is ridiculous that she shouldn't be. One ought not do things that are ridiculous."

"Nurse Robbie is a nursemaid. It is what she is trained to do. Being a governess is not the same."

"She said you are going to ask my mother if you can select a governess for me."

Lady Jonquil brushed one of his hairs away from his eye. "I want to make certain whoever is chosen is wonderful to you."

It seemed he was to have a governess whether he liked it or not. "And did you really ask Nurse Robbie if she would be a nursemaid for your little baby that will be at Brier Hill this year?"

"I did."

"And did my mother really say I could come visit you here sometimes?"

"She did."

He rubbed quickly at his eyes, trying to stop the burning he felt there. "And if Nurse Robbie was here, then I would see her when I visited."

"Yes, you would."

"But she wouldn't get to see Mr. Simpkin?"

"He has to travel about to build his gardens. He couldn't stay here with her."

Adam dropped his gaze to his hands clasped on his lap. "She said she would be very sad when they weren't together."

"She loves him, Adam. Being away from a loved one makes a person sad."

He blinked a few times. "Do you think my mother is sad? I'm away from her."

"I think she is very sad." Lady Jonquil's arm wrapped around him, and she pulled him up beside her. "Your mother loves you, though she doesn't quite seem to know how to show you."

"She makes me go away to the boardinghouse, and she won't come live at the castle, and she says I can't live here with you, and she is making Nurse Robbie go away." His throat hurt with the tears he held back. "All those things make me hurt in my heart. A person oughtn't to make someone she loves hurt in his heart."

"You're right. And I wish I could make all of that hurt go away."

He tucked his head against her, too nervous to look at her as he asked the question weighing heavily on his mind. "Do you love me?"

"I do, so very much. You are family to me, Adam. You always will be."

That was some comfort, though his heart still hurt. "I wish, sometimes, that you were my mother."

"Well, I can be an honorary mother to you. Lord Jonquil's mother is like a mother to me."

"Do you have to call her Lady Lampton?" That didn't seem like a name for a mother.

"I call her Mother Jonquil," she said. "And she calls me Julia."

A surge of excitement pulled his head up. "I could call you Mother Julia."

She squeezed his shoulders. "Oh, I would love that."

He smiled almost without trying. "I would love that too."

"And when I write you letters, I will address them to My Brave Adam because you are the bravest boy I have ever met."

He didn't feel very brave. Nurse Robbie wasn't going to be his nursemaid any longer, and that frightened him. She had always been at the castle. She had always looked after him. When he hadn't felt loved or welcome or wanted, she had promised him he was. When she wasn't there, he wasn't certain he would ever feel safe again. Especially if he wasn't to live at Brier Hill with Mother Julia and Lord Jonquil.

"I cannot call Lord Jonquil Lord Jonquil if you are Mother Julia." Would that mean she wouldn't let him? "What should I call him?"

"The next time you are with him, ask. I am certain the two of you will sort out something you both like."

That was true. Lord Jonquil was very clever, and he had said Adam was as well. With that difficulty sorted, Adam's mind turned back once more to the question he grappled with most.

"If Nurse Robbie works here, I would get to see her?"

"Yes. Every time you visited."

"And if she married Mr. Simpkin and traveled with him to build his gardens, I wouldn't see her very often?"

"Likely not."

Again, the tears he tried to hold back pushed to the surface. "But if she couldn't be with Mr. Simpkin, she would be sad."

In a quiet and soft voice, one that told him Mother Julia understood what he was realizing and knew that it made him ache inside, she said, "I think she would hurt in her heart."

A person oughtn't to make someone he loves hurt in her heart.

"May I stay here while I think about this?" he asked.

Mother Julia pulled the blanket from the foot of her bed. "Lie on the pillow, sweeting. You can lie here and rest. Sleep all night long if you need to. I'll be here to watch over you."

He shifted so he could lay his head on the pillow. She set the blanket over him and tucked him in, as Nurse Robbie used to do before he went to school and became too old for that.

Nurse Robbie needed to go with Mr. Simpkin. He knew she did. But thinking of her going away made him want to cry. Dukes weren't supposed to cry.

Mother Julia brushed her hand over his hair, tenderly stroking it. She hummed a song, though he didn't know what it was. He felt safe with her. That seldom happened.

So he let himself do something he almost never did.

He cried.

Chapter Eighteen

The time arrived for the Twelfth Night celebration at Brier Hill. Adam had been quiet that day, but in a contemplative way rather than a sad one. Robbie wasn't entirely certain what was weighing on him.

She'd been beside herself with worry when discovering, after bearing her troubles to Howard, that Adam hadn't been in his bed. When Lord Jonquil had run him to ground in Lady Jonquil's bedchamber, apparently sleeping quite soundly, Robbie had been more than relieved. She'd been reassured.

Whenever Adam was permitted to spend time at Brier Hill, he'd be loved and he would know he was. And, as Robbie meant to accept Lord and Lady Jonquil's offer of employment until Adam was ready to continue on without her, she could offer him more of that reassurance when he was at Brier Hill.

All the preparations for their celebration were in readiness. Lord Jonquil slipped from the drawing room to fetch his wife, she being the only person in the house who was not privy to the plans for the night.

"Do you think she'll like our party?" Adam asked.

"She will," Robbie said. "I'm certain of it."

He nodded. "I'm glad. I like when she is happy."

Howard stepped up beside Robbie and set an arm around her waist. "It's a fine thing when a man can bring happiness to the womenfolk, i'n' it, Your Grace?"

"It is." Adam gave Howard a conspiratorial look.

"What have I missed?" Robbie asked her sweetheart.

"The menfolk had a discussion in the garden," Howard said, more formally and somberly than was necessary, enough so that she very nearly laughed.

"And you decided that you'd like to see the women in your lives happy?"

He pressed a quick kiss to her cheek. "Always."

She watched Adam for signs of disapproval—he'd not countenanced her growing closeness to Howard the last weeks—but none was forthcoming.

In the next moment, Lady Jonquil and her husband appeared in the doorway of the sitting room. Her curious gaze swept over them all before resting for a moment on the cake, then the homemade crown, then the pile of games and toys.

A smile slowly formed on her face. "Twelfth Night?"

"Adam's idea," Lord Jonquil said.

The lady crossed directly to her tiny houseguest and gave him a quick hug. "Oh, Adam. This is wonderful."

He shuffled his feet, looking down at the tips of his shoes. But spots of pleased color touched his cheeks.

"What are we to begin with?" Lady Jonquil asked.

"The cake," Adam said. "There's a bean in it. We have to find the bean, or we don't know who is in charge tonight."

Lord Jonquil took up the task of cutting and distributing slices of cake. They were all soon in possession of their own. While cake was not quite the rare delicacy in their lives as it had been for many people, they all still took their time and savored the delicious treat.

Slowly, the slices disappeared and the bean had not been discovered. Robbie watched Adam, praying he would find it. She didn't know when next he would get to celebrate Twelfth Night. She wanted this evening to be glorious and enjoyable and a memory he'd carry with him for years to come.

"Lord Jonquil knew where the bean was," Howard whispered to her. "He made certain our little duke's piece contained it."

Aye. This was a family that would love her dear Adam.

Quite suddenly, Adam jumped to his feet. "I found it!" He actually bounced with excitement. "I found it!"

Lord Jonquil fetched the homemade crown and brought it over. He set the crown of evergreen branches and flowers and herbs on Adam's head and offered a deep bow. "Your Majesty."

Adam laughed a little.

"Your Majesty?" Howard also dipped a deferential bow. "May I make a request for the first undertaking of the night?"

Adam nodded, clearly curious.

"I have a gift for Miss Roberta MacGregor, and I'd like to give it to her."

This was news to Robbie

"I think you should," Adam said.

From a hiding place behind a wingback chair, Howard produced a small paper-wrapped parcel. He gave it to her and watched with apparent pleasure as she slowly unwrapped it.

Inside was a wooden brooch carved in the precise shape of a thistle. "You made this, didn't you?"

"After I finished with a certain horse."

Adam's horse, he meant. The one the boy carried about in his pocket.

"Considering the song you sing to our king, here, I thought the thistle a perfect choice," Howard said.

"It's utterly perfect." She clutched it to her heart. "I love it."

He slipped an arm around her waist and kept her tight against him.

"Your Majesty," Lady Jonquil said quite seriously, "it is time for you to select our next activity."

"I decree that next will be shovegroat." Adam played his part a bit too expertly. How easily one could picture him being a very authoritative, perhaps even frightening duke when he was grown. Robbie hoped that tendency would be tempered by his good and compassionate heart.

"We don't have a shovegroat board," Lady Jonquil said.

"Oh, but we do." Howard fetched the board he, Robbie, and Adam had painted the day before.

"Where did this come from?" Lady Jonquil addressed the question to Adam, though her eyes darted to the others as well.

"We made it," Adam said. "Yesterday. I painted the lines—Nurse Robbie said I had to, even though I didn't want to. But she painted the holly and the ivy on it. We thought it would look more like Christmas."

"You both did a fine job." Lady Jonquil gave Adam a quick side hug. He'd refused to be embraced when they'd first arrived at Brier Hill. How much he'd changed in so short a time.

"I don't know how to play the game though." Adam's brow pulled low and tense. "Maybe it isn't fun."

"It is a lark." Lord Jonquil had five coins at the ready and had already plopped himself onto the floor in anticipation of playing the game. He motioned for Adam to join him. "Each player sets a coin at the bottom of the board and then shoves it toward the top." He demonstrated. "If the coin stops between two lines, the player receives the points for that spot."

Adam didn't play for the first couple of rounds, preferring to watch and learn. But even when he did join in, he seemed distracted. His thoughts were elsewhere.

"We can take up a different game," Robbie said. "It's for you to choose."

He pushed out a deep and tense breath. She knew he took any and every responsibility very seriously, but she'd thought he would find that night's assignment enjoyable.

"We need to wassail the tree," Adam said.

To her husband, Lady Jonquil said, "We are taking a *very* traditional approach tonight."

"Except for the Christmas greenery," Lord Jonquil said. "His Majesty has requested it remain up, on account of his being very fond of it."

"Then, it most certainly will."

Even that kindness didn't entirely lift Adam's spirits. Why was he so heavy-hearted? He'd planned the evening's party and had seemed quite excited only the night before.

"Oh, Howard," she whispered to her sweetheart. "I had such hopes that this would be a joyous Christmastime celebration for him."

Howard put an arm around her as they walked toward the walled garden. "I do think he is pleased with our Twelfth Night festivities."

Robbie rested her head against him. "You're telling me I need to have hope?"

"We have a great many things I'm hopeful about, my Robbie. More hopeful than I've been in years and years." He kissed her forehead and squeezed her shoulders. "I know you're nervous for our dear little duke, but I think we've reason to be hopeful for him as well."

They arrived at the newly planted rowan tree, where a bit of wassail and bread awaited their efforts. Adam did look pleased, even if his expression was a bit anxious. Howard kept to Robbie's side, brushed his hand against hers, offered her reassuring smiles. Even with so much uncertainty in her future, Robbie did, in fact, feel hopeful.

The group made short work of the tree-wassailing ceremony, choosing not to include any poems or songs or such.

"That is supposed to make the tree a good tree," Adam told Lady Jonquil. "And it means the people here will have a happy year to come."

"I hope so," she said.

Howard took Robbie's hand. "Hope is a powerful thing," he whispered. "I'm learning that from you, my dear."

Adam looked to Lady Jonquil. She smiled softly, encouragingly. Something unspoken passed between them. Adam's shoulders squared, but he didn't move or speak for a moment. Lady Jonquil gave him a little nudge.

That seemed to be enough.

Adam turned and faced Robbie. "I'm the king tonight, so that means I can make another royal decree."

"I suppose that's true."

"I decree that . . ." He paused. He took a breath. And swallowed. "I decree that you and Mr. Simpkin should get to be happy. And that means when he travels, you should travel with him."

Never could she have guessed he'd say that.

And he wasn't finished. "You can't marry Mr. Simpkin and travel in his coach to build gardens if you're a nursemaid. And you can't be happy with him if you are waiting here for me to visit." His chin quivered, but only for a moment. "I am too old for a nursemaid. And Lucas and Mother Julia's baby would be happy to have you as a nursemaid. But you won't be happy without Mr. Simpkin. And I want you to be happy." His voice broke, but he pushed on. "I wouldn't love you very much if I didn't want you to be happy."

"My dear, wee Adam." Robbie bent down to look him more directly in the eye. "Too many people have left you. I can't join their number. That'd be unkind."

But he shook his head. "You aren't leaving me though. Not like they do. They leave because they don't want to be with me."

That wasn't entirely true, but she was certain it *felt* true to the sweet boy.

"Even when we aren't together," Adam said, "we'll still be family. Family is who you choose."

"And we've chosen each other, haven't we?"

He nodded. "And you should choose Mr. Simpkin."

Robbie twisted and looked up at her beloved Howard. "I really should."

"You really should," Howard said.

"And I have a suggestion of something else the two of you ought to choose," Lord Jonquil said, pulling everyone's attention to him. "We mean to have Adam visit us here whenever he can. And we've every intention of keeping in touch with Mr. Simpkin—I have a very important garden here, after all." He smoothed his cravat and silk waistcoat, making a humorous show of feigned arrogance. "We can send word to the two of you as soon as we know when we are to expect a visit from our favorite duke. When at all possible, you can travel here to Brier Hill to see him."

What a blessing that would be.

Robbie looked to Adam. "What do you say?"

"I would like that." He could be very monarchical when he chose to be. And yet beneath that solemn tone was an eagerness he couldn't entirely hide. "I could tell you about the people at the castle."

"And I could tell you about the places we've traveled," Robbie offered.

He nodded. "And you could sing me the song about the boy the size of a thistle."

Robbie tucked him up close to her. With his handmade Twelfth Night crown and their wassailed tree and the joy of a Christmas celebration fresh around them, she sang.

Saw ye my wee thing? Saw ye my own thing?
Saw ye my bonnie boy down by the lea?
He skipped 'cross the meadow yestere'en at the gloaming.
Small as a thistle my dear boy is he.

Chapter Nineteen

January 1787

Life for Robbie Simpkin was nearly perfect. She and her beloved Howard had traveled the kingdom building gardens and herb sheds and anything Howard was hired to create. They worked side by side, ate many a supper in the gardens they created, and had made a home in their carriage house. The hope she had clung to during their time at Brier Hill now wove through every moment of every day. She had her Howard and was living the life she'd barely allowed herself to dream of.

And they were at Brier Hill again, at the invitation of Lord and Lady Jonquil. Adam would be visiting the kindhearted couple, who had sent word to Devonshire, where Robbie and Howard had been. The heavens were kind, and she and Howard had a gap in work that coincided perfectly. They'd finished the job they'd been undertaking, climbed into their movable house, and made directly for Northumberland.

They were waiting in the entryway, Howard standing with his arms around Robbie. They often stood in precisely that position. Robbie hadn't realized how much she'd wanted to just be held all these years, not until he had come into her life. Their not-actually-Christmas miracle continued to prove itself a blessing.

Lord Jonquil, who had gone to Falstone Castle to fetch their young duke, was expected at any moment. Lady Jonquil paced the entryway, returning repeatedly to the front window, watching for a carriage that had not yet arrived. She held a wee bairn in her arms, one who cooed and gurgled ceaselessly. If Robbie were not mistaken, the newest addition to Brier Hill would grow up to be a very talkative gentleman.

The lady's eyes met Robbie's as she passed her once more. "You likely think me an anxious mess."

"On the contrary, I simply think you've missed our tiny duke."

"Likely almost as much as you have, my dear," Howard said to Robbie.

"He's such a dear lad. How could anyone not miss him when separated from him?"

Lady Jonquil sighed. "I have missed him more than I can say. I wish we could see him more often. I worry that the years will pull him further away from us."

"But he does write to you," Robbie said. "That's a fine thing."

"His letters are as brief and efficient as any I've read before," she said. "How easily I can hear him saying, 'I do not understand the purpose of long, rambling letters.'"

I do not understand the purpose. The only thing Robbie had heard Adam say more often than that over the years she'd been at Falstone Castle was the word *ridiculous*. Oh, how she'd missed him.

"He is, without question," Howard said with a bit of a laugh, "the most efficient child I've ever met."

"I am looking forward to asking him more about this Harry, whom he insists is not his friend but I think very much sounds like one," Lady Jonquil said.

"I watched them when they were at Falstone Castle months ago," Robbie said. "Howard was doing work on the gardens there at the time. Adam has a friend in that boy whether he knows it or not."

"And whether he wants one or not?" Lady Jonquil asked with a laugh.

"I'd wager so, aye."

The bairn in Lady Jonquil's arms watched Robbie intently, the most alert three-month-old she'd just about ever seen.

"May I hold Lord Fallowgill?"

"Of course." As Lady Jonquil set her precious bundle in Robbie's arms, she warned, "He will snatch at every ribbon or ruffle he can wrap his tiny hands around."

"A fashion critic?" Howard asked, a chuckle beneath the question.

"Apparently." Lady Jonquil watched her son fondly.

Robbie met Howard's eye. "Do you see this wee treasure?"

"I do, my dear." Howard had shown himself to have a deep affection for children. "He's a beautiful baby, my lady."

"He has his father's golden curls," Lady Jonquil observed.

"He does at that." Robbie gently ran her fingers over those wisps.

"I cannot thank you enough for the nursemaid you recommended," Lady Jonquil said. "She is a dream."

Robbie tucked the baby up close to her, treasuring the joy of having an infant in her arms again. "And I cannot thank you enough for insisting on the governess chosen for Adam. While I have not met her, knowing you approve of her has given me such peace."

Howard put his arm around Robbie once more. "Has given *both of us* peace."

"And I mean to thank your husband for suggesting Howard work at Falstone Castle for a spell. Being there while Adam was those months ago and before he had a governess meant the boy wasn't so alone."

Whatever response Lady Jonquil might have made was cut off by the sound of hooves and carriage wheels outside. "They've arrived at last!"

Without any of the decorum common to those of her rank, Lady Jonquil threw open the front door and rushed outside. Robbie and Howard followed close behind.

Lord Jonquil was the first to emerge from the traveling carriage. The passing months hadn't dampened his barely controlled energy. He literally hopped down onto the ground, grinning at them all.

"Have you brought him?" Lady Jonquil asked.

"Brought whom?" He made quite a show of being confused.

Behind him, a wee boy, dressed in the solemn and very correct clothing of a young aristocrat, stepped regally from the carriage, his gaze finding Lady Jonquil before anyone else, allowing Robbie to study him without him knowing she was. His black hair was pulled back in a ribbon matching his coat. His shoes were polished to a high shine. His appearance was impeccable and far closer to that of a forty-nine-year-old than an almost-nine-year-old. There was no mistaking her little Adam. He was a bit taller, a bit older, appeared a bit more solemn, but he was still himself.

"Oh, my Adam!" Lady Jonquil rushed to him and pulled him into a fierce embrace. "My dear, brave Adam! You are here at last."

"Lucas refused to ask the driver to go faster." The accusation was offered quite seriously, but Lord Jonquil's grin told anyone witnessing the moment that Adam was teasing him.

"Oh, Lucas, do fetch Philip," Lady Jonquil said. "I want Adam to meet him."

Lord Jonquil crossed to Robbie, blocking her view of her wee Adam. He indicated his son in her arms. "I know he's difficult to give up, but do you mind if I steal this little peapod from you?"

"Promise I can hold him again," she said, "and I won't kick up a fuss."

"You have my solemn vow."

Lord Jonquil took his son and moved back toward his wife and the little boy they had all but adopted, who was turned away from Robbie, fully consumed in the greetings he was receiving from this generous couple.

Howard pulled Robbie into a tender and affectionate embrace. "He looks happy, Robbie. And he seems quite sure of himself. More so than when we last saw him."

She leaned against her beloved husband. "He is growing up."

"No longer as tiny as a thistle."

"He is also no longer alone," she said. "And neither am I."

"Life's been good to us, my Robbie."

Across the way, Adam was eyeing the infant Lord Jonquil held. He didn't seem to know what to say or do with a baby, but he was quite content to lean against "Mother Julia" and listen to all she had to say about tiny Philip, Lord Fallowgill.

"Now, Adam, I will set aside my motherly gushing and suggest you make the 'good day' that is several months in the making."

He looked up at Lady Jonquil, clearly confused.

"There is someone standing not far from here, watching all this," she said. "We've kept you so distracted that you haven't spotted her yet." Lady Jonquil motioned to where Robbie and Howard stood.

Adam turned and looked in the direction Lady Jonquil had indicated. His greeting would, Robbie didn't doubt, be very sedate and proper. That had been very much his way when they'd last parted. It appeared to be even more so now.

To her delighted shock, he grinned and ran directly to her, calling out, "Nurse Robbie!"

In an instant, she was holding her beloved boy to her, clutching him tight, and silently blessing the heavens for moments like these.

From within her embrace, Adam said, "Mr. Simpkin, you're here as well." And he sounded truly pleased.

"I'd not miss seeing you for all the world, Your Grace." Howard set a hand on Adam's back and his other arm around Robbie. "It wouldn't be a Twelfth Night celebration without you here."

Adam leaned back and looked into Robbie's eyes, excitement dancing in his. "Is it Twelfth Night?"

"Tomorrow," she said. "We have plans to decorate the house in greenery, gather all the games we can think of—"

"Wassail the tree?" Adam asked eagerly.

"Of course," Howard answered.

"And eat cake," Lord Jonquil added, he and his family having joined them.

"And crown a monarch," Lady Jonquil said.

Adam looked at all of them, smiling and happy and, at last, hopeful. "And we'll be together. That is the best part of Christmas. The very best part."

Their Christmas miracle continued to be a blessing, and life was, indeed, very, very good.

Bonus Epilogue

December 1791

ADAM HAD DISCOVERED VERY QUICKLY during his first year at Harrow that it was tradition for fathers to visit their sons at school, a tradition he had been told continued at Oxford. He'd resigned himself immediately to not being part of that. And he'd told himself firmly that he didn't care.

But Lucas had, without Adam saying a word about any of it, visited him multiple time at Harrow. He'd worried a little that Lucas and Mother Julia would forget about him as the years passed. They didn't live at Brier Hill any longer, and they had four children of their own now. He didn't entirely know how to make sense of their continued presence in his life.

That confusion, however, did not prevent him from accepting the invitation Lucas had extended when he'd arrived at Harrow a couple of days before school recessed for Christmas. Adam would be spending the festive season at Lampton Park.

He'd not had a Christmas with his honorary family in four years. He'd visited them at Lampton Park, just not as part of the holy season. That the prospect made him as nervous as it did eager was a frustrating thing.

He was thirteen years old now, hardly a baby. Yet he was acting embarrassingly infantile.

"It's a shame Harry couldn't make the journey with us," Lucas said. "I suspect the three of us could have some legendary larks at the Park."

"I don't have larks." That might disappoint Lucas, but Adam didn't think it fair to mislead him.

"Ah, but I've been dreaming of a Highwayman's Christmas for years." Lucas's eyes danced about the way they always did when he teased Adam. No one ever teased him but Lucas. Everyone else was too afraid, which was a very useful thing.

"I was a little ridiculous during that first visit to Brier Hill."

"You were brilliant." Lucas Jonquil had a penchant for jests and amusing absurdity, but he also allowed people to see when he was being sincere.

While Adam appreciated being the recipient of that openness, he knew he could never match it. Another thing that would likely disappoint Lucas.

"I didn't know you would be inviting me to spend Christmas at Lampton Park," Adam said. "I don't have a present for Mother Julia."

Lucas grinned evermore broadly. "Don't you realize, Adam? You are the present."

"I am?"

"I have been anticipating for weeks the look on her face when she realizes you are with me. You and I are soon to be legends in the annals of Jonquil Family Christmases."

When she realizes . . . A worrisome realization followed close on that declaration. "She doesn't know I'm returning with you?"

"Julia has been entirely jealous of my visits to Harrow to see you, but she worries that if you were being visited by a lady who mothers you as much as she does, you might be ridiculed for it."

"No one ridicules me." Adam had made perfectly sure of that. It had taken a shocking amount of fisticuffs and an unwillingness to back down from any challenge, but life at Harrow was easier now that everyone was too afraid of him to torture him. "Will I be an inconvenience to her?"

"To Julia?" Lucas shook his head as if the very idea were entirely absurd. "Not at all."

"What about your mother? She lives at Lampton Park."

"And she tucks herself cozily in at the Dower House whenever she wishes for time to herself. She'll not be the least vexed."

Adam had met the dowager countess during his previous visits, but he'd not felt the same closeness to her as he did to Lucas and Mother Julia. Truth be told, he didn't feel the same closeness to anyone as he did to them.

A mere moment later, Lampton Park came into view. Adam wanted to feel excited, but he was still feeling inarguably anxious. He was not at all accustomed to the feeling, and he didn't overly like it.

The carriage stopped at the front portico. The moment the door was open, Lucas eagerly jumped out. Adam didn't have to guess why—the answer presented itself. Two little boys with golden curls just like Lucas's rushed from the house with shouts of "Papa!" and were scooped up by their father.

"You were gone for seven hundred years, Papa," the older of the two said.

"Not seven hundred," the other objected. "But lots."

"I was fetching a Christmas surprise for your mother." Lucas kissed them each on their cheeks, holding them close and bouncing them excitedly. "Where are the twins?"

"We are faster than they are," the older boy proudly declared.

Adam watched from the shadows of the carriage interior. The Jonquil family was always loving and affectionate. Seeing that was one of the things he appreciated about being with them.

"You are going to need two more arms, Lucas."

Mother Julia.

Adam sat up at the sound of her voice, leaning a little more toward the door so he could see her better. He'd missed her. Being near her again tugged fiercely at his heart. It was too dark inside for him to be spotted, and he liked that: being able to feel things but not be seen feeling them.

She was walking slowly toward Lucas with two tiny boys, the twins, toddling beside her. Was she truly going to be pleased that he was there? Her family had grown so much since that first Christmas. There wasn't really a need for him any longer.

Lucas turned to his oldest boy, still in one of his arms. "They are walking faster than they used to. They'll be able to keep pace with you soon enough."

"Papa, I don't have to be fastest. I am in charge." The little boy's dramatic tone brought a smile to his father's face.

"Time to trade hugs." Lucas set his older two boys on their feet once more, then took his twins in his arms. "My sweetings." He kissed their cheeks, just as he had the other boys.

"It is almost Christmas, Papa," one of the twins said. "Grandmother likes Christmas. And Mama likes Christmas. And we like Christmas."

Throughout the more vocal boy's declaration, his twin silently and enthusiastically nodded.

"I am glad you're excited," Lucas said, "because so am I."

Watching him with his sons turned Adam's anxiousness to a sadness, though he wasn't sure why. Their interaction didn't elicit grief-filled reminders of his late father. Adam loved his father, and his father had loved him, but they hadn't often exchanged hugs, and neither of them had used pet names. His feelings were something different.

Mother Julia managed to quickly kiss Lucas even with his arms full of children and two more clinging to his legs. "You were gone longer than expected. Did you have an errand beyond London?"

"I did." The mischief in Lucas's voice eased some of the heaviness in Adam's heart. "I was fetching your Christmas present." And quick as that, Adam was nervous again.

"Considering you left me here for nearly a fortnight with four boys who wanted nothing more than to have their nearest parent run with them for hours on end,"—there was too much of a laugh in her voice for the complaint to be a serious one—"this Christmas present you diverted course for had best be something truly magnificent."

"My dear," Lucas said, "this present is one I will reference for years as a means of getting myself out of your black books."

Mother Julia laughed. "I like when you inevitably land yourself in trouble; I get the most wonderful apology presents."

"This one, sweetheart, isn't an apology. It's simply because I love you both."

"Us both?"

Lucas looked back through the open carriage door. His arms full, he twitched his head in a clear instruction for Adam to disembark.

I am the Duke of Kielder, Adam reminded himself. *I am not a coward.*

He squared his shoulders and moved to the open carriage door. Mother Julia pulled in a sharp breath. Adam stepped out, frustrated with himself for being too nervous to look at her. If she was disappointed, seeing it would hurt too deeply for him to endure.

"Oh, my Adam." She threw her arms around him and hugged him in the fierce and firm embrace he'd come to associate with his beloved substitute mother. "I have missed you."

He, who never hugged anyone, returned the offering. And for the first time in ages, he breathed.

Christmas Eve

Adam only ever played games when he was with Lucas. And he was always surprised to discover he was not only good at them, but he also enjoyed taking part in them. He sometimes felt as though he were a different person when he was with Lucas and Mother Julia.

They had gathered the Christmas greenery that morning, before the boys had taken their midday naps, something Mother Julia said Philip, her oldest son, only pretended to participate in. The drawing room was festively decorated, and the family was enjoying a rousing game of huckle buckle beanstalk.

Adam was part of it all.

In fact, the item they were searching for was the carved horse Mr. Simpkin had given him during that long-ago Christmas at Brier Hill. Though he wouldn't have admitted it to anyone beyond this family, Adam took it with him whenever he was away from Falstone. He felt less lonely with that reminder of such a happy time in his life.

Layton, the second oldest, approached Adam with a look of frustration. "Where did Papa hide the horse? I cannot find it."

Did all four-year-olds pout like that?

"I don't know where it is hidden," Adam said. "I am looking for it as well."

He wasn't as comfortable with children as he wished he were. He'd done his best to follow Lucas's lead with them, but Adam hadn't the same boundless energy or penchant for playfulness. He also wasn't one for hugs and sweet smiles and softness, like Mother Julia. Still, he thought the four little boys liked him, a miracle fit for the holy season.

Lucas snatched little Layton up. "Adam is not going to help you cheat." He tickled the boy, sending him into a fit of giggles.

The two-year-olds were playing a game of their own, running nonstop around the room. Jason identified everything they passed. Corbin nodded his agreement.

Philip marched over to the sofa beside Adam and tossed himself dramatically onto the cushions. "If I don't find the horse, Christmas will be ruined!" His eyes darted to Adam, clearly checking to see if his performance had the desired effect.

"I have had a great many Christmases ruined, Lord Jonquil. This won't manage it, I assure you."

The little boy climbed up onto the sofa and looked up at him. His golden brows pulled in an expression of focused concern. "Why have your Christmases been ruined?"

"I don't have a father or mother to play games with me."

"Who do you play games with?"

Adam hadn't expected an interrogation from a five-year-old. "With no one. That is why my Christmases are not as merry as yours."

"Mama." Philip remained on the sofa but turned to face his mother. "Adam Grace doesn't have anyone to play games with him. He needs to stay with us so he can play games on Christmas."

The little lordling had taken to calling him "Adam Grace," though Adam hadn't determined yet whether the boy was genuinely confused by his parents calling their visitor Adam while the staff all called him "Your Grace" or if the boy was using the misnomer in order to be funny.

"Adam is staying with us for Christmas, Philip," Mother Julia said. "Your papa brought him to Lampton Park specifically to be here at Christmas."

Philip turned wide eyes on Adam. He dropped his voice to a vehement whisper. "Tomorrow is Christmas."

"I know." Did he actually think Adam didn't know what day it was? There was a lot Adam didn't understand about children.

The little boy stood on the sofa and, with a posture and tone that would not be out of place on any stage in London, declared dramatically, "We have to stop playing huckle buckle beanstalk."

Lucas, who had Corbin under an arm and was chasing Jason, to the delight of both his twins, asked, "Why do we need to stop?"

"Adam Grace is staying for Christmas, Papa." Philip set his fists on his hips. "He has to be part of the surprise."

"Surprise?" Mother Julia looked to Lucas with wide-eyed curiosity.

Philip slapped his hands over his mouth, clearly fearing he would reveal a secret.

Layton filled in the silence, though he addressed his father, not his mother. "Adam is one of Mama's boys. He has to be part of the Christmas surprise."

"Right." Lucas assumed a somber demeanor and walked to Adam. "Carry this one." He held out Corbin in the manner one would hand over a portmanteau, which, for reasons Adam didn't understand, made the tiny boy laugh again.

Adam eyed Corbin with misgiving that he knew he didn't keep hidden. "I don't have experience with children."

"Precisely why I'm having you hold the one least likely to bite."

"Bite?"

"A small chance of it, and a small bite at that." Lucas's somber expression dissolved quickly.

"Lucas will tease you mercilessly if you let him, Adam," Mother Julia said.

Adam knew that well enough. He found it a little confusing, but he liked it just the same.

With a smile, Lucas set Corbin's feet on the ground. "Hold Adam's hand," he instructed his boy. "Jason, take the other one."

The small twins tugged Adam to his feet.

"And I am not to be told what this excursion is that you all are undertaking?" Mother Julia didn't actually seem upset to be excluded. It was more of this family's tendency to tease.

"It is a surprise," Layton declared firmly, and that was the end of the conversation.

Adam, tugged along by the twins, followed Lucas, flanked by Philip and Layton, out of the drawing room.

"I am not actually one of her boys, you know." He felt he ought to point that out before he was pulled into anything he had no right to be part of.

Lucas stopped and turned back to look at him. "Do you truly think that because you don't live here or because we don't share a surname or a family tree, you aren't one of our boys? I taught you about family, Adam, and I taught you better than that."

"Family is who you choose." Adam repeated the lesson Lucas had ingrained in him during that long-ago Christmas celebration.

"And we aren't ever going to unchoose you, Adam Boyce. Not ever." He shrugged. "Even if you decide to unchoose us, it won't do you any good. I know where you live."

Unchoose them? Adam never would. Never could.

"The surprise, Papa." Philip tugged impatiently on his father's coattail.

Lucas raised an eyebrow. Under his breath, he said to Adam, "In case you were wondering who is truly in charge in this house."

"I've known it from the moment I met your oldest five Christmases ago."

Lucas laughed as his son dragged him onward. They continued all the way to the library.

When they entered the large room, Lucas said to Philip, "Go fetch it," and the boy rushed without hesitation to a chairside table.

The little Lord Jonquil pulled open the drawer and, rising up on his toes, reached inside. He pulled out a leather box.

Lucas motioned for Adam to join him on the long sofa. He did so, and the boys climbed up, Corbin sitting on Adam's lap, which shocked him.

Philip sat in the middle of them all and very solemnly said, "We've made Mama a treasure box, and we've all put treasures in it."

"Things she considers treasures or things you consider treasures?" Adam asked.

None of the children seemed to understand the question, so Adam looked at Lucas.

"Whatever they think she will be happy to find in the box," he explained. "It is an . . . eclectic collection so far."

"You have to put something in it too," Philip said. "You are one of Mama's boys. You have to give her a treasure."

"I don't have anything to give her." It had been one of Adam's worries during the journey to Nottinghamshire.

Lucas slipped an arm around his shoulders and squeezed. "You'll think of something. I have complete faith in you."

Christmas Day

"Mama. Mama. Mama. Mama. Mama."

Mother Julia met her oldest's eyes. "Philip."

Understanding slid over his features. He took a deep breath and slowly released it. Adam had seen him do precisely that a few times during his visit. He suspected the boy had been given very specific instructions on what to do when he was overly excited.

"It's Christmas, Mama," Philip said, nearly all his exuberance now firmly in place. "You have to have your Christmas surprise."

"I have been very excited about this Christmas surprise," Mother Julia said. "I can hardly wait to discover what it is."

"It's a treasure box!" Layton exclaimed.

"Layton." Philip scolded his brother. "You can't tell her what the surprise is. You're ruining it."

"I didn't tell her what was in it," Layton shot back.

"It's a treasure box. She will know it has treasure in it."

"Treasure comes in many forms," Adam said. "She will still be surprised. No need to come to blows."

With no more reassurance than that, the two oldest set aside their quarrel, rushing away together to collect the treasure box, which Lucas had brought into the room earlier.

Mother Julia, who sat beside Adam, patted his hand. "Well done, Adam. You handled that brilliantly."

"I think I am getting better at knowing what to do with children. I never interact with any."

She squeezed his hand. "You'll simply have to come visit us more often. We have plenty."

He met her eyes. Feeling a little foolish for the emotional admission yet unable to leave it unspoken, he said, "I would like that very much."

She smiled so softly, the same smile he had learned to love almost immediately during that first Christmas with her and Lucas. "So would I."

Philip and Layton arrived directly in front of her and dropped the leather box on her lap. They bounced with excitement. Corbin and Jason were distracted with climbing all over their father, Jason offering a running commentary and Corbin nodding along. It was the usual approach for them both.

Mother Julia opened the box. Her two oldest sons could not have looked more excited. Adam, to his frustration, was nervous again. He didn't like feeling upended or unsure of himself.

She pulled a toy soldier out, one quite a bit worse for the wear. "Oh, Layton. This is your favorite soldier."

"Your brother was a soldier," Layton said, leaning against her legs.

"Yes, he was."

"This soldier is like him. You can think about your brother."

Mother Julia leaned to him and gave him a quick motherly kiss. "It is perfect, my little Layton. Will you keep hold of him for me?"

Layton nodded, accepting the offered toy.

She next pulled out a small bundle wrapped in cloth and tied with twine. She tugged at one end of the bow, untying it. The fabric fell open, revealing a half dozen ginger biscuits.

"Jason and Corbin insisted on those," Lucas said. "Even they know ginger biscuits are your favorites."

"Thank you, my sweet boys," she said to them, though they didn't seem to be paying much attention, busy as they were climbing on their father as if he were an obliging tree. Lucas appeared to be in heaven.

Mother Julia took the topmost biscuit and broke it in half, giving one half each to Layton and Philip. She held out the second biscuit to Adam.

"These are your treasures," he objected.

"The people in this room are my treasures." Just as when he'd been eight years old, her loving, welcoming smile soothed much of the ache he carried with him.

He accepted the biscuit, but he was too discomposed to eat it.

"Look at mine next." Philip tapped the leather box.

Mother Julia pulled out a long ribbon in a pretty shade of green-tinted blue. "Is this from you?"

Philip nodded. "It was at Grandmother's house, but it is the same color as your cloak, so it should be for you."

"It is the same color." Mother Julia tied it in a loose loop around her neck, almost like a piece of jewelry. "I'll wear it like this for now, sweeting."

Her oldest smiled broadly, clearly quite proud of himself. "Now look at Adam Grace's."

Mother Julia looked at him once more. "Did you put a treasure in here for me?"

He nodded. "But it isn't anything impressive, certainly nothing that can be considered a treasure."

"You think too poorly of yourself, my Adam. You are a remarkable person, wonderfully thoughtful, resilient, and, as I've been telling you for five years now, incredibly brave."

"I try to be all those things," he said.

"You succeed."

"Look at Adam Grace's treasure," Philip demanded. "It is part of the Christmas surprise."

Mother Julia reached inside the box and pulled out *The History of Little Goody Two-Shoes*.

"You have your own children now. You can read it to them." He was proud of his steady voice. He didn't know if Mother Julia would appreciate his offering, but it had been one of his most cherished possessions for five years now. Giving it to her so her boys could have the same tender moments he'd had listening to her read it hurt more than a little. But he hid that with the fierce expertise he had gained over the last half decade. "They would enjoy having you read it to them. I know they would."

"You had it with you at Harrow?" she asked.

He nodded. Like the carved horse, he always took Mother Julia's book with him wherever he went.

"And you want my boys to be read the story?"

Adam swallowed with some difficulty. "I am too old for it now."

Mother Julia had given the book as a show of love. Letting it go felt like losing some of his connection to her. He could hardly bear it. But she would be happier if her sons were happier. Mother Julia was the one who had taught him that loving someone meant wanting them to be happy.

She scooted closer to him on the sofa. She took his hand in his, her other hand resting on the book on her lap.

"Do you remember, Adam, that first Christmas when you gave Nurse Robbie the gift of building a life with her darling Mr. Simpkin, free of guilt or worry over you?"

"I wanted her to be happy." It had hurt though. It still did sometimes.

"I hear from her now and then, and she is happy."

"I'm glad." He'd missed her horribly that first year. And he still thought of her and wished he could see her more often. But she was happy and loved.

That was what he wanted for her, she who had loved him at a time when he'd felt very alone.

"You gave her that, my wonderful, brave Adam. I hope you realize how remarkable that is, how remarkable you are."

Mother Julia always managed to make him feel less alone and less overwhelmed. She was remarkable.

"What I would love from this treasure"—she tapped the book—"is if, when you are visiting us, you would read it to the boys."

"You want me to read it?"

"Older brothers often read to their younger brothers the books their parents read to them."

He couldn't help a hopeful flip of his heart. "I'm not their older brother," he reminded her.

"You are one of my boys, Adam Boyce, and I would love for you to read this story to my little boys." She sounded sincere, and he didn't think she was speaking out of pity. "That means you will need to bring it with you when you visit."

Bring it with him. "I am to keep it?"

"This will be Adam Grace's story, the one they get to hear from you. I would love that. I would love for all of you to have that special connection."

She set the book on his lap. He laid his free hand on it, relief washing over him, knowing he wouldn't lose it. But more even than that, he felt hopeful.

"I'll have to visit a few times to get through the story," he warned.

She leaned closer and, in a conspiratorial whisper, said, "Part of your gift to me, Adam."

"Did you like our treasure box, Mama?" Layton asked, walking his toy soldier on the floor by her feet.

"I love it," she said. "And I love all you boys."

Adam hoped he truly would always be included in that count. While the little ones ran about rambunctiously, he remained on the sofa beside the lady who had filled such an enormous hole in his heart these past years, watching the gentleman who had done the same.

"I am so grateful you're here with us, Adam," Mother Julia said.

"And I am grateful Nurse Robbie brought me to Brier Hill five years ago. It was, without question, a life-altering gift."

"For us as well," she said. "It brought you into our lives, and we love you so dearly."

"Family is who you choose," Lucas said to him. "And we will choose you forever."

Nurse Robbie hadn't allowed Adam to turn down the invitation that had brought him to Brier Hill, no matter that he'd argued with her about it. She had brought him to their home when he'd been lonely, grieving, and lost in so many ways. And they had loved him ever since.

Mother Julia had praised the gift he'd given Nurse Robbie. But even as heartrendingly difficult as that sacrifice had been, he was and always would be indebted to her for what she had given him.

Family. Hope. And love.

About the Author

Sarah M. Eden is a *USA Today* best-selling author of more than seventy witty and charming historical romances, which have sold over one million copies worldwide. Some of these include 2020's Foreword Reviews INDIE Awards gold winner for romance, *Forget Me Not*, 2019's Foreword Reviews INDIE Awards gold winner for romance, *The Lady and the Highwayman*, and 2020 Holt Medallion finalist, *Healing Hearts*. She is a three-time Best of State gold-medal winner for fiction and a three-time Whitney Award winner.

Combining her obsession with history and her affinity for tender love stories, Sarah loves crafting deep characters and heartfelt romances set against rich historical backdrops. She holds a bachelor's degree in research and happily spends hours perusing the reference shelves of her local library.

Sarah is represented by Pam Pho at Steven Literary Agency.

www.SarahMEden.com
Facebook: facebook.com/SarahMEden
Instagram: @sarah_m_eden